Die DomSpitzen

(The DomPeaks)

Written by
Martin "PeeWee" Cordemann

"Rudolph and Leopold"
was created by
Guido and Ralf Paul

Artwork by
Ralf Paul

Inking by
Adriano Honorato Lucas

Idea, conception and realization by

IDEENSCHMIEDE Paul & Paul

www.ipp-world.de

Coloring by
Adriano Honorato Lucas, Ralf Paul

Translated by
Christine Stockebrand

City Comics

Die DomSpitzen

Glück-Auf-Str. 278
46284 Dorsten
www.konturblau.de
1st edition, July 2007
Published by: Konturblau Verlag

ISBN: 978-3-939565-03-1
Printed by: Westermann Druck Zwickau GmbH

SWOOOOSH!!!
SWERVE!
SPIRAL!
SPIN!
SWOOOSH!!!
CRASH!
SUMM!!!
SSUMMMM!!!
SSUMMMM!!!
SWOOOSH!!!
TÄNGLE!!!

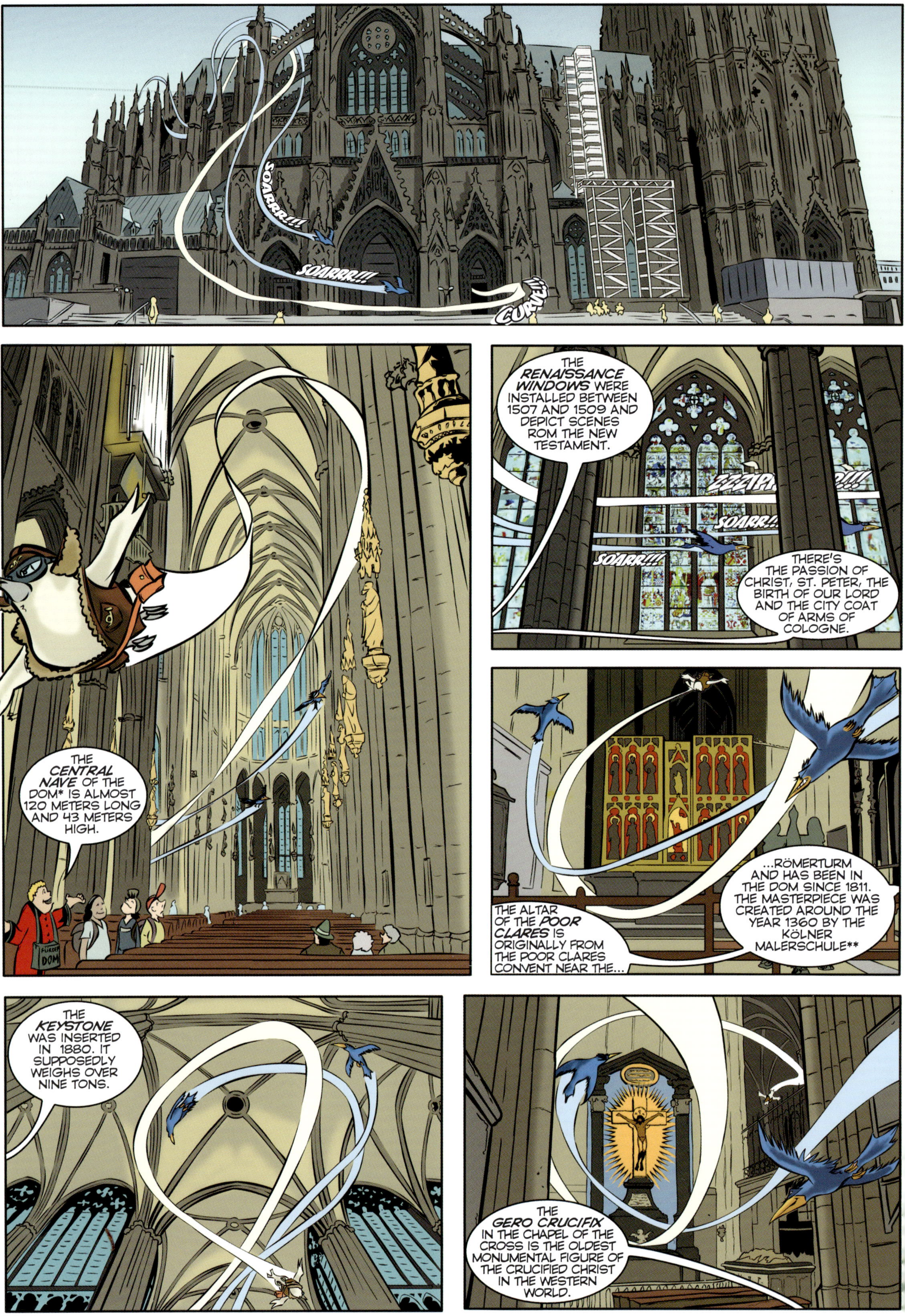
SOARRR!!!
SOARRR!!!
CURVE!!!
THE CENTRAL NAVE OF THE DOM* IS ALMOST 120 METERS LONG AND 43 METERS HIGH.
THE RENAISSANCE WINDOWS WERE INSTALLED BETWEEN 1507 AND 1509 AND DEPICT SCENES ROM THE NEW TESTAMENT.
SOARR!!
SOARR!!!
THERE'S THE PASSION OF CHRIST, ST. PETER, THE BIRTH OF OUR LORD AND THE CITY COAT OF ARMS OF COLOGNE.
THE ALTAR OF THE POOR CLARES IS ORIGINALLY FROM THE POOR CLARES CONVENT NEAR THE...
...RÖMERTURM AND HAS BEEN IN THE DOM SINCE 1811. THE MASTERPIECE WAS CREATED AROUND THE YEAR 1360 BY THE KÖLNER MALERSCHULE**
THE KEYSTONE WAS INSERTED IN 1880. IT SUPPOSEDLY WEIGHS OVER NINE TONS.
THE GERO CRUCIFIX IN THE CHAPEL OF THE CROSS IS THE OLDEST MONUMENTAL FIGURE OF THE CRUCIFIED CHRIST IN THE WESTERN WORLD.

* *Cologne Cathedral*

** *Cologne Art movement in the Middle Ages*

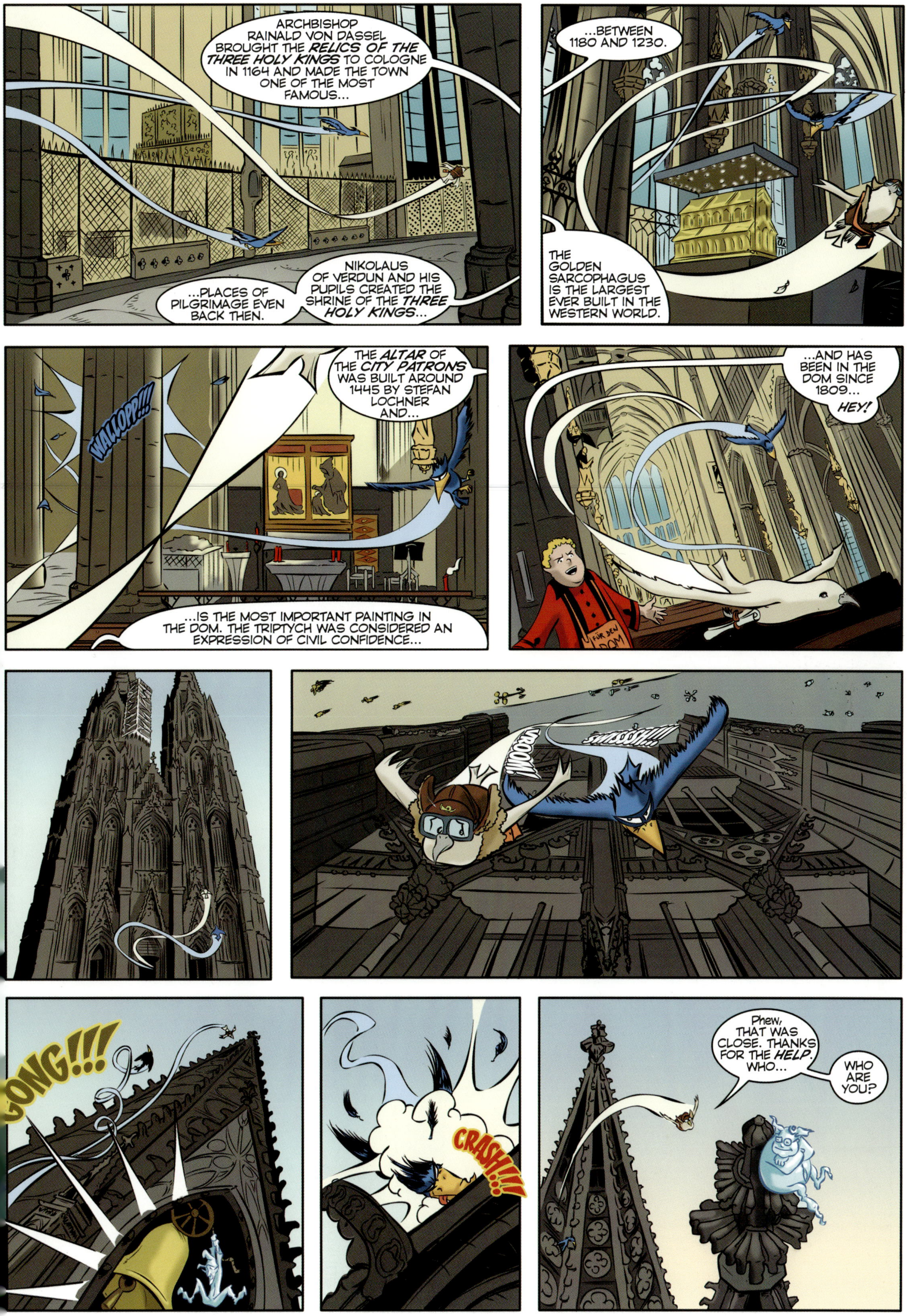
ARCHBISHOP RAINALD VON DASSEL BROUGHT THE *RELICS OF THE THREE HOLY KINGS* TO COLOGNE IN 1164 AND MADE THE TOWN ONE OF THE MOST FAMOUS...
...PLACES OF PILGRIMAGE EVEN BACK THEN.
NIKOLAUS OF VERDUN AND HIS PUPILS CREATED THE SHRINE OF THE *THREE HOLY KINGS*...
...BETWEEN 1180 AND 1230.
THE GOLDEN SARCOPHAGUS IS THE LARGEST EVER BUILT IN THE WESTERN WORLD.
WALLOPP!!!
THE *ALTAR* OF THE *CITY PATRONS* WAS BUILT AROUND 1445 BY STEFAN LOCHNER AND...
...IS THE MOST IMPORTANT PAINTING IN THE DOM. THE TRIPTYCH WAS CONSIDERED AN EXPRESSION OF CIVIL CONFIDENCE...
...AND HAS BEEN IN THE DOM SINCE 1809...
HEY!
FÜR DEN DOM
VROOM!
SWISSSH!!!
ONG!!!
CRASH!!!
Phew, THAT WAS CLOSE. THANKS FOR THE *HELP*. WHO...
WHO ARE YOU?

WE ARE THE DOMSPITZEN!
THE... DOMPEAKS? WHAT DOES THAT MEAN?
WE ARE THE GUARDIANS OF THE DOM!
GUARDIANS OF THE DOM? SO WHAT DOES THAT MEAN? ARE YOU HUMAN? ARE YOU GHOSTS? ARE YOU CATHOLICS?
WE ARE GHOSTS...
...BUT WE USED TO BE HUMAN...
...MANY YEARS AGO...
1235 A. C.
...THOSE WERE THE DAYS. EMPEROR FRIEDRICH II. HAD JUST BEEN IN TOWN. AND HIS FUTURE WIFE, THE ENGLISH PRINCESS ISABELLA...
WHAT'S THAT GOT TO DO WITH IT?
NOTHING, BUT THOSE WERE GREAT DAYS!
HANG ON, HANG ON... THAT WAS THE YEAR 1235, AND YOU WERE GHOSTS?!
NO, WE WEREN'T GHOSTS!
NOT YET...
1248 A. C.
...WE WERE SUPPOSED TO DO SOME WORK FOR THE ARCHBISHOP OF COLOGNE, KONRAD OF HOCHSTADEN.
WE WANT TO BUILD A BEAUTIFUL, NEW CATHEDRAL HERE.
IT WAS AN EASY JOB!
BUT WE DON'T WANT TO BUILD IT FROM NOTHING.
IN ORDER TO SAVE MONEY I INSTRUCT YOU TO TEAR DOWN ONLY THE EASTERN PART OF THE OLD DOM...
...AND LEAVE THE WEST WING THE WAY IT IS.
SO, WE ERECTED A PROTECTIVE WALL, WE HOLLOWED OUT THE EASTERN PART OF THE WALLS AND PUT PLENTY OF WOOD IN THEM SO THAT EVERYTHING ABOVE IT WOULD COLLAPSE. THAT'S...
...HOW IT WAS DONE IN THOSE DAYS
WHAT DO YOU THINK?
IT SHOULD DO!
IT WAS APRIL AND IT WAS COLD AND WE THOUGHT, LET'S EARN A BIT MORE ON THE SIDE...
YOU CAN SLEEP HERE, BUT ONLY FOR ONE NIGHT. TOMORROW, THIS THING IS COMING DOWN

LET'S...
...WARM...
...IT...
...UP A...
...LITTLE!
SHIVER!
SHIIIVER!
SHAKE!
SHAKE!
CHATTER!
CAN'T HARM
— shiver —
IT WILL BE TORN DOWN ANYWAY TOMORROW!
shiver
— YES —
shake!
SNOOOORE!
ZZZZZZZ!
DREAM!
CRACKLE!
BURN!!!
FLAME!!!
ROOOOAAAR!!!
LEOPOLD? RUDOLPH?
WHERE ARE YOU??
WE ARE... DEAD!?
ARE YOU CRAZY? WE...
OH, YOU'RE RIGHT!
OH WELL, OFF TO HEAVEN THEN.
DO YOU THINK THEY HAVE...
HANG ON!

NOT SO FAST!
DON'T YOU THINK I KNOW WHAT YOU HAVE DONE? YOU BURNT DOWN THE DOM...
...ALL OF IT!
BUT THAT WASN'T ENOUGH, NO, YOU ALSO HAD TO TAKE THE...
...MONEY OF THE POOR FOLKS...
THEY DIED BECAUSE OF YOU! YOU'VE GONE TOO FAR! BUT NO-ONE WILL EVER KNOW WHAT DESPICABLE DEED YOU HAVE COMMITTED AND THAT PEOPLE HAD TO DIE.
IN ORDER TO PAY FOR YOUR DEEDS YOU WILL MAKE SURE THAT THE NEW DOM WILL BE COMPLETED! YOUR PUNISHMENT WILL BE EXTENDED FOR...
...EVERY MISHAP THAT OCCURS. AND FOR EVERY MISHAP YOU CAN AVERT, YOU WILL BE SPARED A YEAR! IF YOU LEAVE THE DOM AND SOMETHING HAPPENS IN YOUR ABSENCE, YOU WILL IMMEDIATELY BE CALLED BACK TO THE DOM!
DO YOU UNDERSTAND?
YES.
YES.
15th August 1248
I AM DELIGHTED TO LAY THE FOUNDATION STONE OF THE NEW DOM.
INCREDIBLE! YOU MUST HAVE MET SO MANY INTERESTING PEOPLE OVER TIME...
NO. WE CAN ONLY TALK TO ANIMALS. WE ARE INVISIBLE TO EVERYBODY ELSE.
BUT... YOU MUST BE VERY LONELY!
WELL, WE HAVE US...
Sigh!
AND THEN THE DOM WAS BUILT.
MAN, YOU MUST HAVE BEEN UP TO A LOT OF MISCHIEF, IF YOU'RE STILL HERE. SO, HOW LONG DOES IT TAKE TO BUILD A DOM? TWO, THREE YEARS?!
OH, I WISH...
27th September 1322
C'MON RUDI, DON'T EXAGGERATE! WE DIDN'T LIVE IN A WOOD ENGRAVING!
27th September 1322

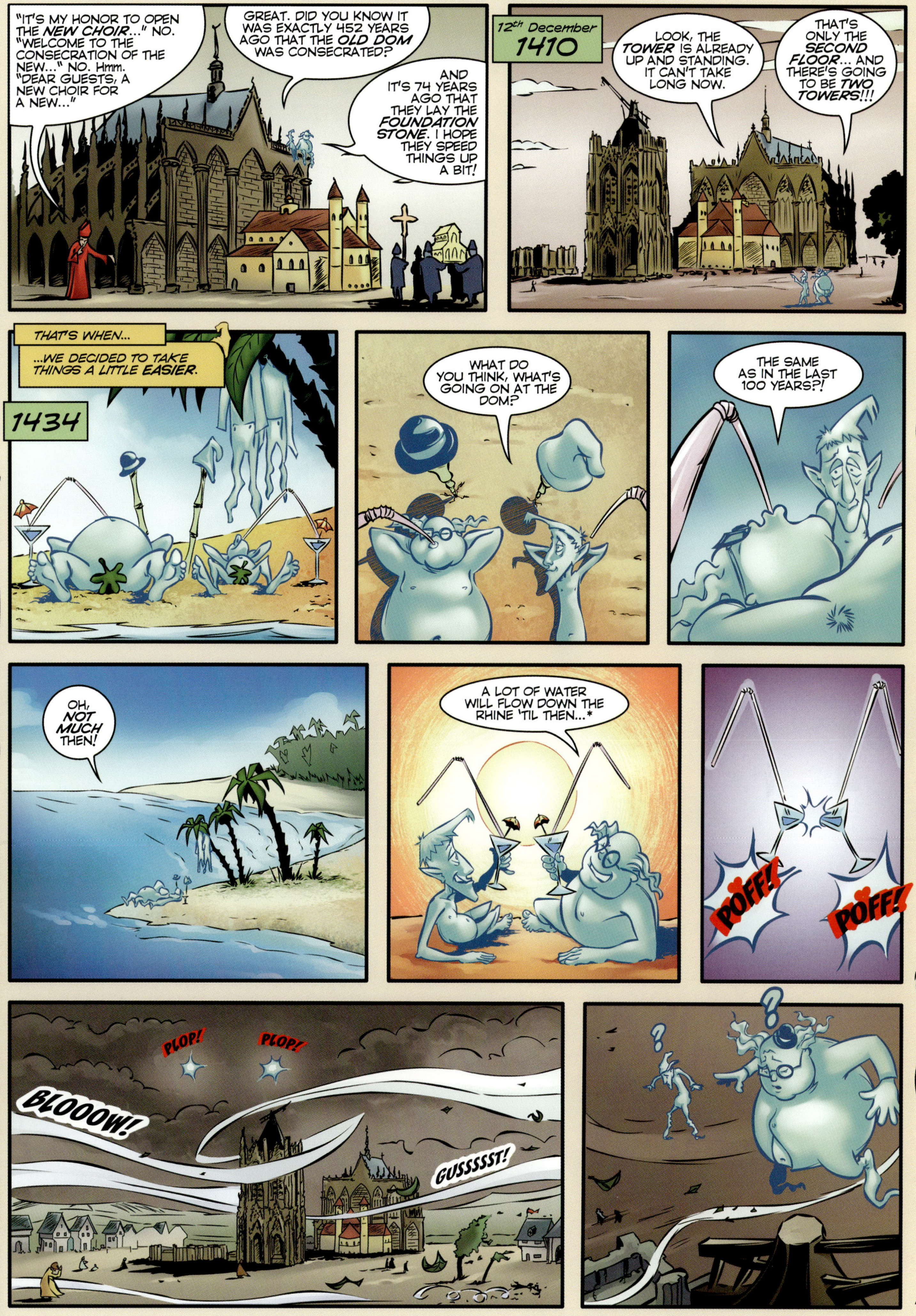
"IT'S MY HONOR TO OPEN THE NEW CHOIR..." NO. "WELCOME TO THE CONSECRATION OF THE NEW..." NO. Hmm. "DEAR GUESTS, A NEW CHOIR FOR A NEW..."
GREAT. DID YOU KNOW IT WAS EXACTLY 452 YEARS AGO THAT THE OLD DOM WAS CONSECRATED?
AND IT'S 74 YEARS AGO THAT THEY LAY THE FOUNDATION STONE. I HOPE THEY SPEED THINGS UP A BIT!
12th December
1410
LOOK, THE TOWER IS ALREADY UP AND STANDING. IT CAN'T TAKE LONG NOW.
THAT'S ONLY THE SECOND FLOOR... AND THERE'S GOING TO BE TWO TOWERS!!!
THAT'S WHEN...
...WE DECIDED TO TAKE THINGS A LITTLE EASIER.
1434
WHAT DO YOU THINK, WHAT'S GOING ON AT THE DOM?
THE SAME AS IN THE LAST 100 YEARS?!
OH, NOT MUCH THEN!
A LOT OF WATER WILL FLOW DOWN THE RHINE 'TIL THEN...*
POFF!
POFF!
PLOP!
PLOP!
BLOOOW!
GUSSSSST!
?
?

* Famous Cologne song.

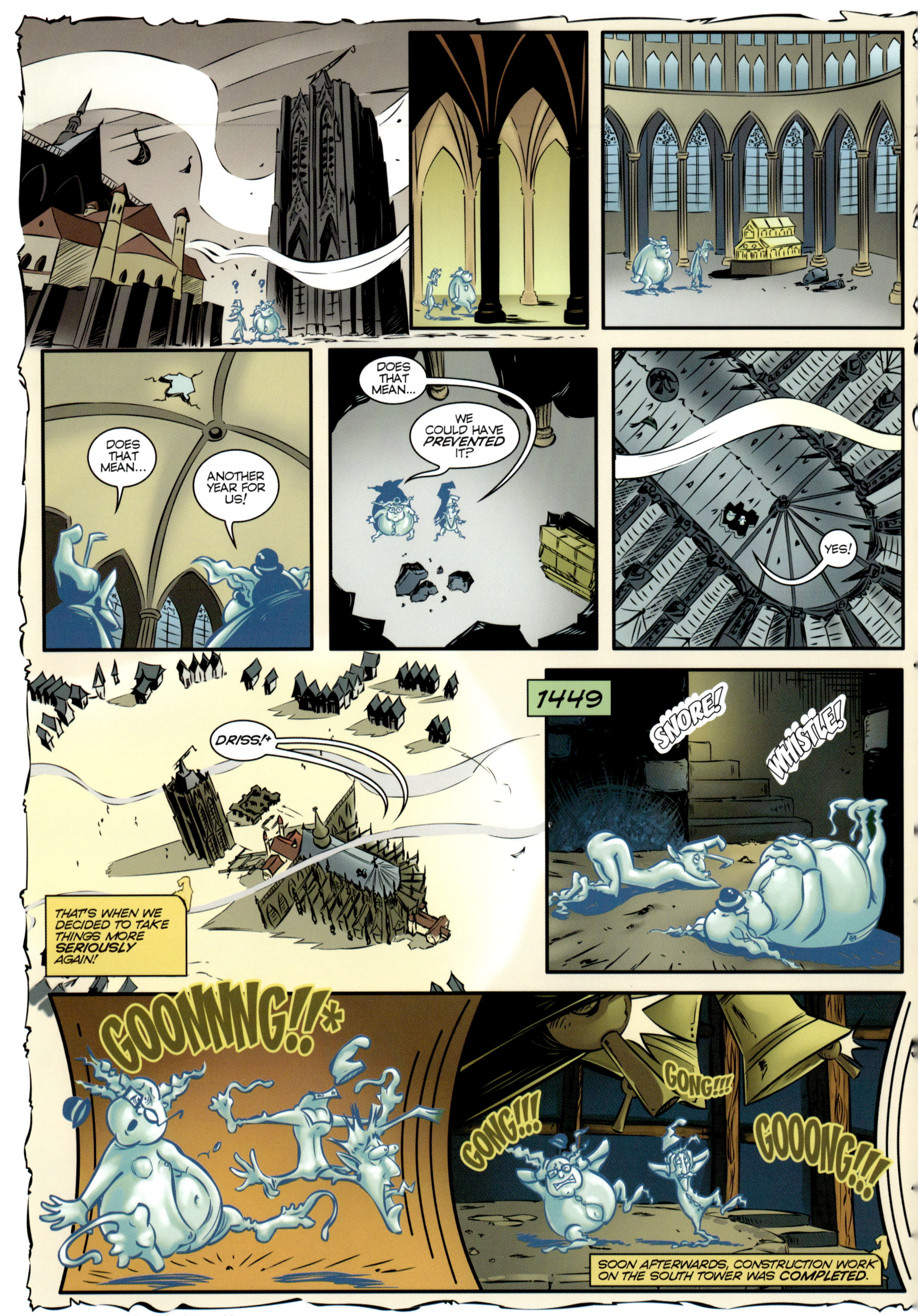
DOES THAT MEAN...
ANOTHER YEAR FOR US!
DOES THAT MEAN...
WE COULD HAVE PREVENTED IT?
YES!
DRISS!+
THAT'S WHEN WE DECIDED TO TAKE THINGS MORE SERIOUSLY AGAIN!
1449
SNORE!
WHISTLE!
GOONNNG!!*
GONG!!!
GONG!!!
GOOONG!!!
SOON AFTERWARDS, CONSTRUCTION WORK ON THE SOUTH TOWER WAS COMPLETED.

+ Cologne dialect for 'Damn'!
* The Bell of the Magi, the "Speciosa" and the "Pretiosa" (which was the largest bell in former Europe) make up the most tremendous peal of bells ever to be heard in the Western World.

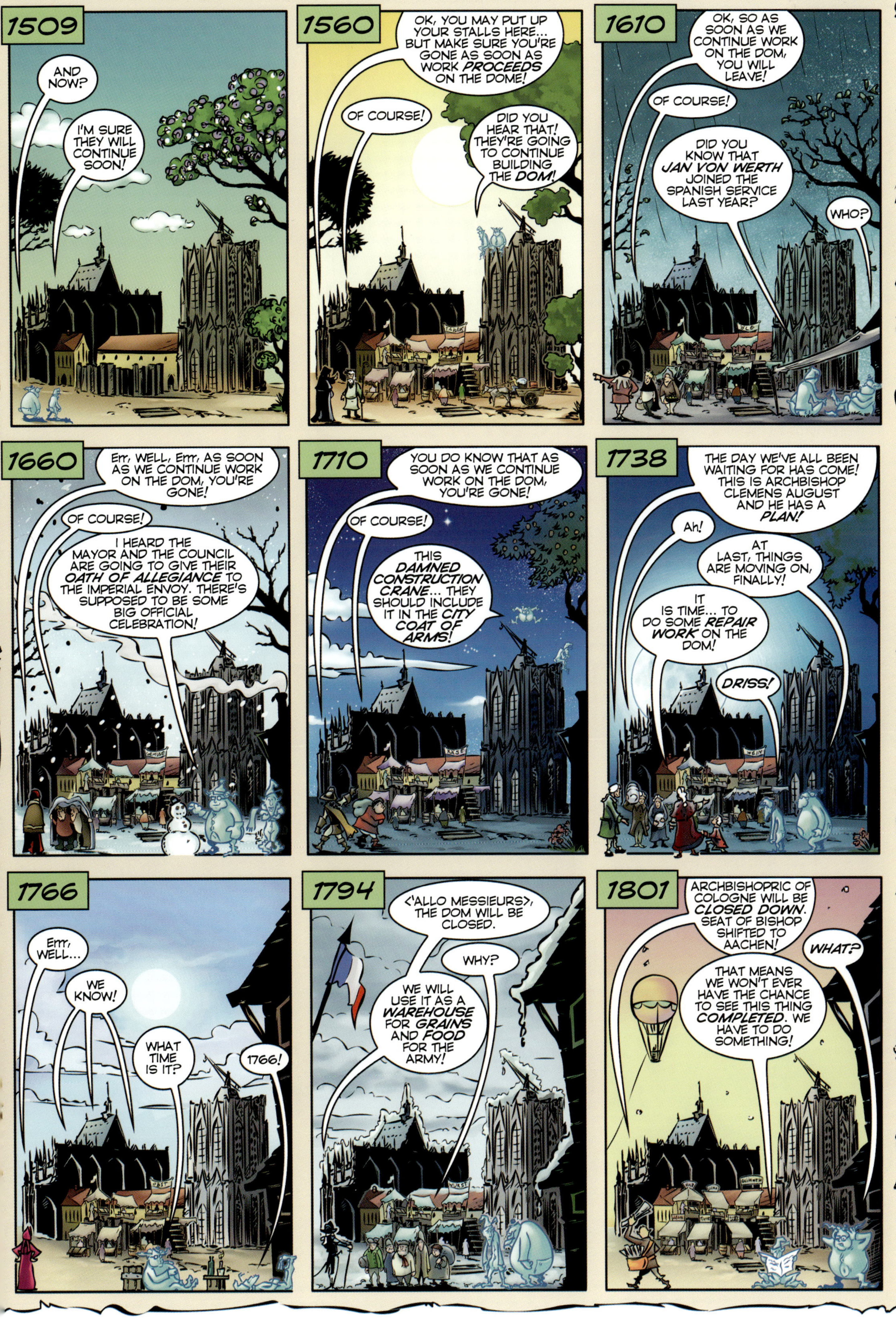
1509
AND NOW?
I'M SURE THEY WILL CONTINUE SOON!
1560
OK, YOU MAY PUT UP YOUR STALLS HERE... BUT MAKE SURE YOU'RE GONE AS SOON AS WORK PROCEEDS ON THE DOME!
OF COURSE!
DID YOU HEAR THAT! THEY'RE GOING TO CONTINUE BUILDING THE DOM!
1610
OK, SO AS SOON AS WE CONTINUE WORK ON THE DOM, YOU WILL LEAVE!
OF COURSE!
DID YOU KNOW THAT JAN VON WERTH JOINED THE SPANISH SERVICE LAST YEAR?
WHO?
1660
Errr, WELL, Errr, AS SOON AS WE CONTINUE WORK ON THE DOM, YOU'RE GONE!
OF COURSE!
I HEARD THE MAYOR AND THE COUNCIL ARE GOING TO GIVE THEIR OATH OF ALLEGIANCE TO THE IMPERIAL ENVOY. THERE'S SUPPOSED TO BE SOME BIG OFFICIAL CELEBRATION!
1710
YOU DO KNOW THAT AS SOON AS WE CONTINUE WORK ON THE DOM, YOU'RE GONE!
OF COURSE!
THIS DAMNED CONSTRUCTION CRANE... THEY SHOULD INCLUDE IT IN THE CITY COAT OF ARMS!
1738
THE DAY WE'VE ALL BEEN WAITING FOR HAS COME! THIS IS ARCHBISHOP CLEMENS AUGUST AND HE HAS A PLAN!
Ah!
AT LAST, THINGS ARE MOVING ON, FINALLY!
IT IS TIME... TO DO SOME REPAIR WORK ON THE DOM!
DRISS!
1766
Errr, WELL...
WE KNOW!
WHAT TIME IS IT?
1766!
1794
<'ALLO MESSIEURS>, THE DOM WILL BE CLOSED.
WHY?
WE WILL USE IT AS A WAREHOUSE FOR GRAINS AND FOOD FOR THE ARMY!
1801
ARCHBISHOPRIC OF COLOGNE WILL BE CLOSED DOWN. SEAT OF BISHOP SHIFTED TO AACHEN!
WHAT?
THAT MEANS WE WON'T EVER HAVE THE CHANCE TO SEE THIS THING COMPLETED. WE HAVE TO DO SOMETHING!

WAIT A MINUTE! ARE YOU SAYING...
...THAT THEY HAVEN'T WORKED ON THE DOM FOR CENTURIES?!
...THAT THE CONSTRUCTION CRANE STOOD THERE FOR OVER 400 YEARS?!
....ARE YOU SAYING THE DOM WAS WHITE?!
SIGH!
YES, THE DOM WAS WHITE!
1807
WE HAD TO DO SOMETHING!
THEY SHOULD TEAR THE WHOLE THING DOWN!
JUST TEAR IT DOWN, THE DOM.
TEAR IT DOWN? YOU KNOW WHAT WILL HAPPEN TO US THEN?
STAY CALM!
YES, YOU'RE RIGHT. THIS IS A DISGRACE!
AAPEFOTT!+ I'LL SHOW 'EM!
LET'S SEE, WHAT WE CAN DO AGAINST IT!
YOU KNOW WHAT THE WORST THING IS THAT WE CAN DO TO THESE ADVERSARIES OF THE DOM?
NO, WHAT?
IF THEY WERE MADE FRIENDS OF THE DOM!
SULPIZ BOISSERÉE
MELCHIOR BOISSERÉE
SULPIZ, IF SOMETHING CANNOT BE COMPLETED...
...IT HAS TO BE REMOVED!
I DON'T KNOW, MELCHIOR...
I'M STUCK WITH THIS DRAWING!
!

+ Cologne dialect for Idiot!

HEY!
WHAT WAS THAT FOR?
MAYBE... MAYBE SOME THINGS *SHOULD BE* COMPLETED!
THAT YEAR, HE MADE SURE THAT THE FRENCH GOVERNMENT GRANTED *19.652 FRANCS* FOR THE IMPROVEMENT ON THE DOM RUIN!
1811
AND THAT WAS ONLY THE BE-GINNING. *GOETHE* WAS THERE...
A *BEAUTIFUL* DOM. BUT... WHAT IS THE *KERNEL* OF THE BRUTE?
?
1814
...THE PRUSSIAN CROWN *PRINCE FRIEDRICH WILHELM* WAS THERE...
VERY NICE!
BUT WHY IS THE CONSTRUCTION *TAKING SO LONG?*
WE COULD DO WITH A KING *LIKE THAT!*
...JUST *ONE* THING WAS *MISSING!*
FINALLY, WE CAN *PROCEED* WITH THE CONSTRUCTION OF THE DOM!
YES! ...BUT WHERE ARE THE *CONSTRUCTION PLANS?*

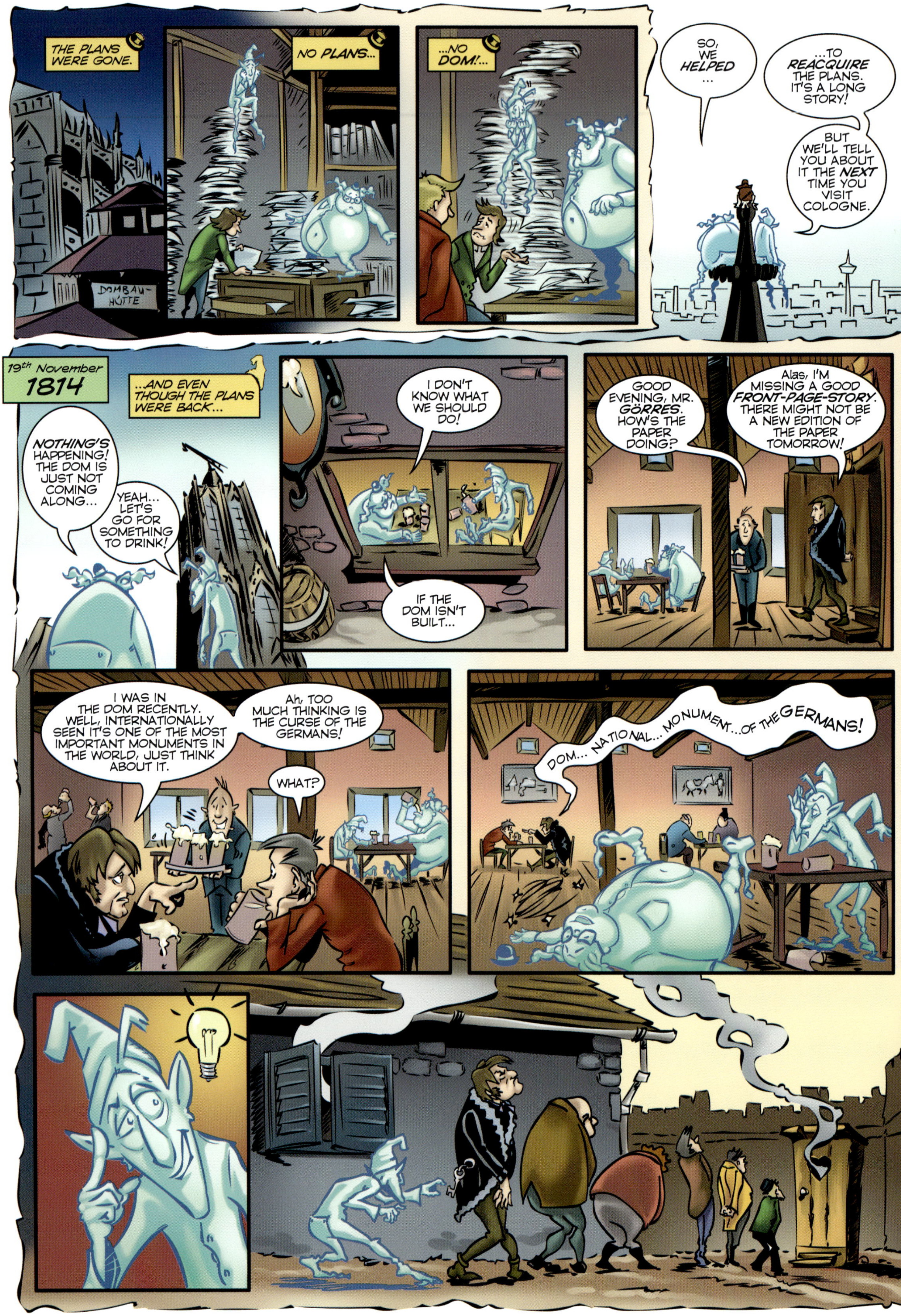
THE PLANS WERE GONE.
DOMBAU-HÜTTE
NO PLANS...
...NO DOM!...
SO, WE HELPED ...
...TO REACQUIRE THE PLANS. IT'S A LONG STORY!
BUT WE'LL TELL YOU ABOUT IT THE NEXT TIME YOU VISIT COLOGNE.
19th November 1814
...AND EVEN THOUGH THE PLANS WERE BACK...
NOTHING'S HAPPENING! THE DOM IS JUST NOT COMING ALONG...
YEAH... LET'S GO FOR SOMETHING TO DRINK!
I DON'T KNOW WHAT WE SHOULD DO!
IF THE DOM ISN'T BUILT...
GOOD EVENING, MR. GÖRRES. HOW'S THE PAPER DOING?
Alas, I'M MISSING A GOOD FRONT-PAGE-STORY. THERE MIGHT NOT BE A NEW EDITION OF THE PAPER TOMORROW!
I WAS IN THE DOM RECENTLY. WELL, INTERNATIONALLY SEEN IT'S ONE OF THE MOST IMPORTANT MONUMENTS IN THE WORLD, JUST THINK ABOUT IT.
Ah, TOO MUCH THINKING IS THE CURSE OF THE GERMANS!
WHAT?
DOM... NATIONAL... MONUMENT...OF THE GERMANS!

RHEINISCHER MERKUR
WHAT DO WE NEED THE KEY FOR?
IT'S A SURPRISE!
FINISHED!
AND THE *KEY*?
CLICK!
AH, THE NEW EDITION OF THE *MERKUR*!

BRAUHAUS zum schlafenden KRAN
?
WHAT THE...?
RHEINISCHER MERKUR
20th November 1814
THE COLOGNE DOM
A NATIONAL MONUMENT OF GERMANY THAT NEEDS TO BE COMPLETED!
by Joseph Görres
1823... or 1833
WE WERE THINKING ALONG THE RIGHT TRACK. WE HAD TO MAKE THE DOM A SYMBOL FOR EVERYONE, SO THAT PEOPLE WOULD HELP TO COMPLETE THE BUILDING.
HOWEVER, PROGRESS WAS VERY SLOW.
THE REPAIR WORKS BEGAN...
REPAIRS CONTINUED...
UNTIL ONE DAY...
7th June 1840
DO YOU REMEMBER THE CROWN PRINCE? THE ONE WHO LIKED THE DOM SO MUCH?
YES.
HE'S THE KING NOW!
THIS PRESENTED A WHOLE NEW RANGE OF POSSIBILITIES. IF WE DID IT PROPERLY...
WE'LL GO TO THE KING!
WHAT?
WE HAVE TO CONVINCE THE KING THAT THE DOM NEEDS TO BE COMPLETED. WE TRIED EVERYTHING ELSE. THIS IS OUR LAST CHANCE.
AND HOW DO YOU KNOW, WHERE THE KING IS?
I'M SURE WE'LL FIND HIM!

Aachen, 1840
Koblenz, 1840
GOOD MORNING, HERR REICHENSPERGER.
Munich, 1841
Vienna, 1841
AND WE'RE EVEN IN THE WRONG COUNTRY!
Mainz, 1841
Magdeburg, 1841
Alas, THIS IS USELESS. BERLIN IS NEXT ON THE LIST.
AND WHAT ARE THE CHANCES...
...OF THE KING BEING THERE?
DID YOU LOSE SOMETHING?
OH... IT DOESN'T MATTER ANYMORE.
C'MON, DON'T BE SAD. AT LEAST WE TRIED!
LET'S GO FOR A DRINK!

The Cologne Dom and Germany's unity
The Dom is the most significant stronghold, Germany will not let it perish, will not let it fall until the patriotic stream will have absorbed the very last drop of Germanic blood.
DID YOU SEE THIS? THE KING GAVE HIS PERMISSION FOR THE FOUNDATION OF A CENTRAL CATHEDRAL ASSOCIATION!
IT'S HARD TO BELIEVE. HELP ORGANIZATIONS FOR THE DOM ARE BEING ESTABLISHED ALL OVER GERMANY! YES, THE DOM IS AN IMPORTANT ELEMENT FOR THE DEVELOPMENT OF THE ENTIRE GERMAN NATION!
WHAT?
12th January 1842
Ah, HOME AT LAST. AND THERE IT IS, THE DOM. JUST AS WE LEFT IT...
WE DIDN'T FIND THE KING. WE DIDN'T FIND THE CAPITAL CITY. WE DIDN'T ACHIEVE ANYTHING. WE DIDN'T...
AND JUST AS IT'LL ALWAYS BE. IT'S HEART-BREAKING!
WE DID IT!
THE KING ORDERED THE COMPLETION OF THE DOM BY ROYAL COMMAND!
4th September 1842
AND FINALLY, THERE IT WAS: THE FOUNDATION STONE CEREMONY FOR THE FURTHER CONSTRUCTION OF THE DOM.
I PROMISE THAT UNTIL THE DOM'S COMPLETION 50.000 TALER FROM THE STATE TREASURY WILL BE PAID EVERY YEAR - IF THE CENTRAL CATHEDRAL ASSOCIATION RAISES THE SAME AMOUNT OF MONEY.
THE DOM SHALL BE A NATIONAL MONUMENT FOR ALL GERMANS.
ALAAF COLOGNE!*
WHAT A GREAT MOMENT! BUT WHERE IS THE ARCHBISHOP?
HE WAS ARRESTED!

* Alaaf: Cologne salute during Karneval

1847
FROM THEN ON, EVERYTHING WENT WELL...
WE HAVE A PROBLEM. THE CENTRAL CATHEDRAL ASSOCIATION IS NOT MAKING ENOUGH MONEY.
...SO THE CONSTRUCTION WAS...
...ONCE AGAIN...
...IN A DANGEROUS CRISIS...
...THAT LASTED UNTIL 1855.
1855
THE KING ARRIVED ONE LAST TIME.
AND SLOWLY THE BUILDING OF THE DOM CONTINUED...
1860
...THE ROOF WAS COMPLETED...
WHAT'S THAT STRANGE SMOKE?
IT'S COMING FROM THE NEW MAIN STATION!
1863
...THE INTERIOR WAS FINISHED...
I THINK THE SMOKE IS DAMAGING THE FACADE!
OH GREAT!
1864
...AND MONEY POURED IN AGAIN!
FOLKS, BUY LOTTERY TICKETS, TICKETS FOR THE DOM! THE PROCEEDS WILL GO TO THE BUILDING OF THE TOWERS!
DOMBAU LOTTERIE
WHAT'S ALL THIS THEN?
THE KING GAVE THE CENTRAL CATHEDRAL ASSOCIATION THE PERMISSION FOR A DOM LOTTERY THAT COULD BE HELD EVERY YEAR.
AND FINALLY WE MADE IT...
YOU MEAN THE DOM WAS COMPLETED?
NO, THE TOWERS WERE FINALLY THE SAME HEIGHT!
28th February 1868
AND FINALLY, FINALLY THAT SILLY OLD CRANE THAT HAD BEEN COLOGNE'S LANDMARK FOR MORE THAN 500 YEARS WAS REMOVED!
I WILL MISS IT.
I WON'T!
10 YEARS LATER THE EMPEROR DONATED A BELL TO THE DOM, THE EMPEROR'S BELL.
IT WAS AWESOME...
...ALTHOUGH IT NEVER SOUNDED RIGHT. ONLY REACHED THE C-NOTE YEARS LATER. 1909, I THINK.
I BELIEVE THE BELL WAS THE PERFECT EXAMPLE FOR A SENSIBLE USE OF WEAPONS, BECAUSE IT WAS MOLDED FROM 22 FRENCH CANNONS.
WHAT HAPPENED TO IT?
OH IT WAS MELTED DOWN AGAIN IN 1918 - TO MAKE WAR MATERIAL!
15th October 1880
BUT THEN...
...ON THE BIRTHDAY OF EMPEROR WILHELM'S BROTHER WHO LAID THE FOUNDATION STONE FOR FURTHER PROGRESS ON THE DOM IN 1842...
...THE DOM WAS FINALLY COMPLETED!

THERE WAS A PROCESSION - JUST LIKE KARNEVAL!*
KLING!
HOW HIGH IS THE DOM NOW?
157,38 METERS!
BUT - THAT MAKES IT THE HIGHEST BUILDING IN THE WORLD!
WE CELEBRATED FOR THREE DAYS.
WHAT A GREAT MOMENT!
BUT WHERE IS THE ARCHBISHOP?
HE WAS ARRESTED!
BUT IF THE DOM WAS FINISHED, WHY ARE YOU GUYS STILL HERE?
WELL, THE DOM WASN'T COMPLETELY FINISHED. THE MOSAIC FLOOR, FOR INSTANCE, WASN'T READY UNTIL 1898.
AND THEN WE CAME ACROSS A FEW... COMPLICATIONS!
20th May 1906
AND YOU RECKON NOTHING CAN GO WRONG?
I MEAN, WHAT CAN HAPPEN NOW?
LOOK AT THAT!
AT LEAST THEY MANAGED TO COMPLETE THEIR BUILDINGS!
WE REALLY DESERVED THIS HOLI...
POFF!
POFF!
PLOP!
PLOP!
...DAY!
WHAT'S THE MATTER NOW?
IT... IT JUST CAME OFF AND FELL DOWN!
SO WE MADE SURE THINGS LIKE THAT NEVER HAPPENED AGAIN.
OH YES, WE KEPT GUARD AND PROTECTED THE DOM.
NOT EVEN THE SMALLEST WINDOW BROKE. THE DOM WAS FINISHED AND INTACT! UNTIL...

* Cologne Mardi-Gras

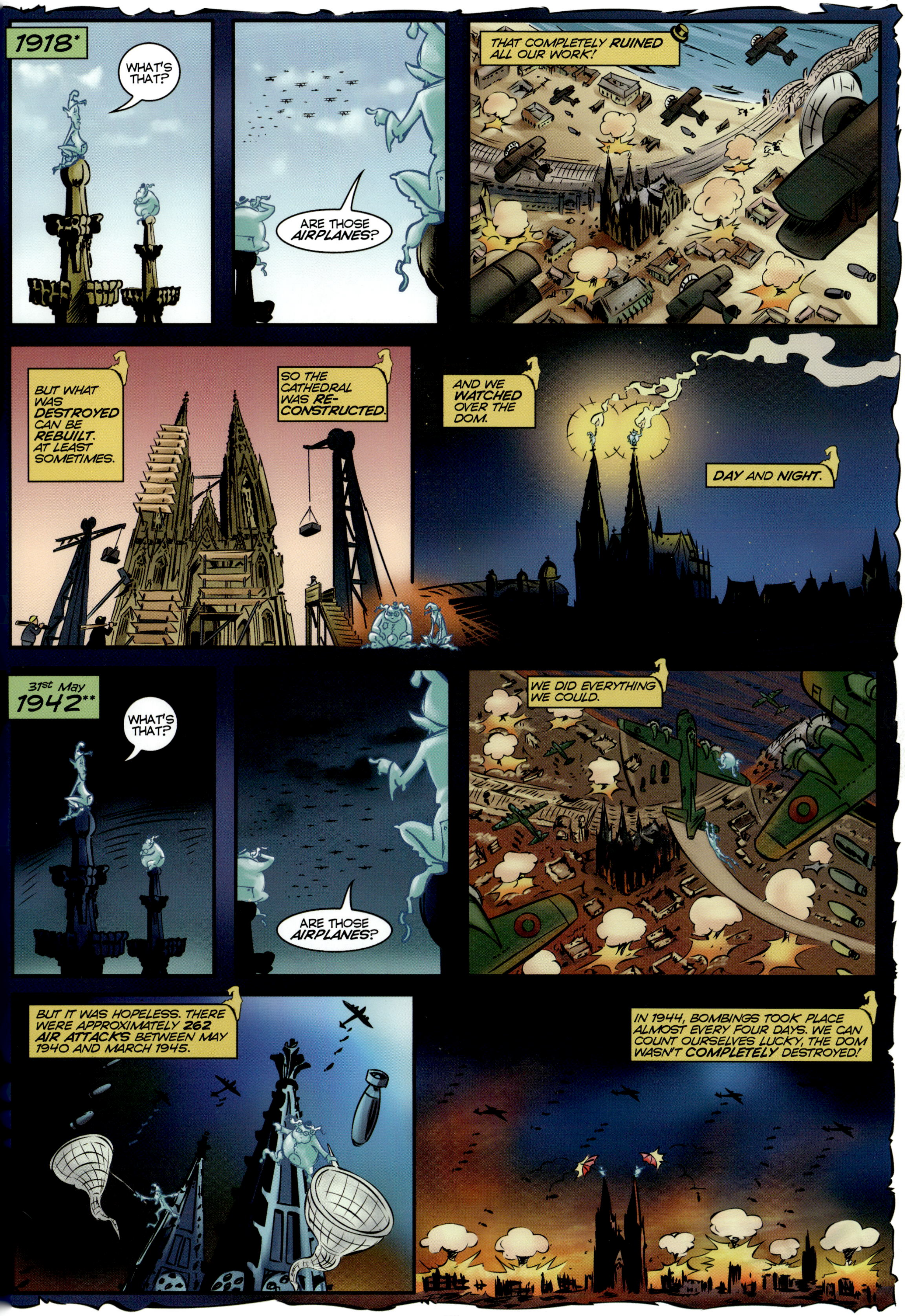
1918*
WHAT'S THAT?
ARE THOSE AIRPLANES?
THAT COMPLETELY RUINED ALL OUR WORK!
BUT WHAT WAS DESTROYED CAN BE REBUILT. AT LEAST SOMETIMES.
SO THE CATHEDRAL WAS RE-CONSTRUCTED.
AND WE WATCHED OVER THE DOM.
DAY AND NIGHT.
31st May 1942**
WHAT'S THAT?
ARE THOSE AIRPLANES?
WE DID EVERYTHING WE COULD.
BUT IT WAS HOPELESS. THERE WERE APPROXIMATELY 262 AIR ATTACKS BETWEEN MAY 1940 AND MARCH 1945.
IN 1944, BOMBINGS TOOK PLACE ALMOST EVERY FOUR DAYS. WE CAN COUNT OURSELVES LUCKY, THE DOM WASN'T COMPLETELY DESTROYED!

* First World War ** Second World War

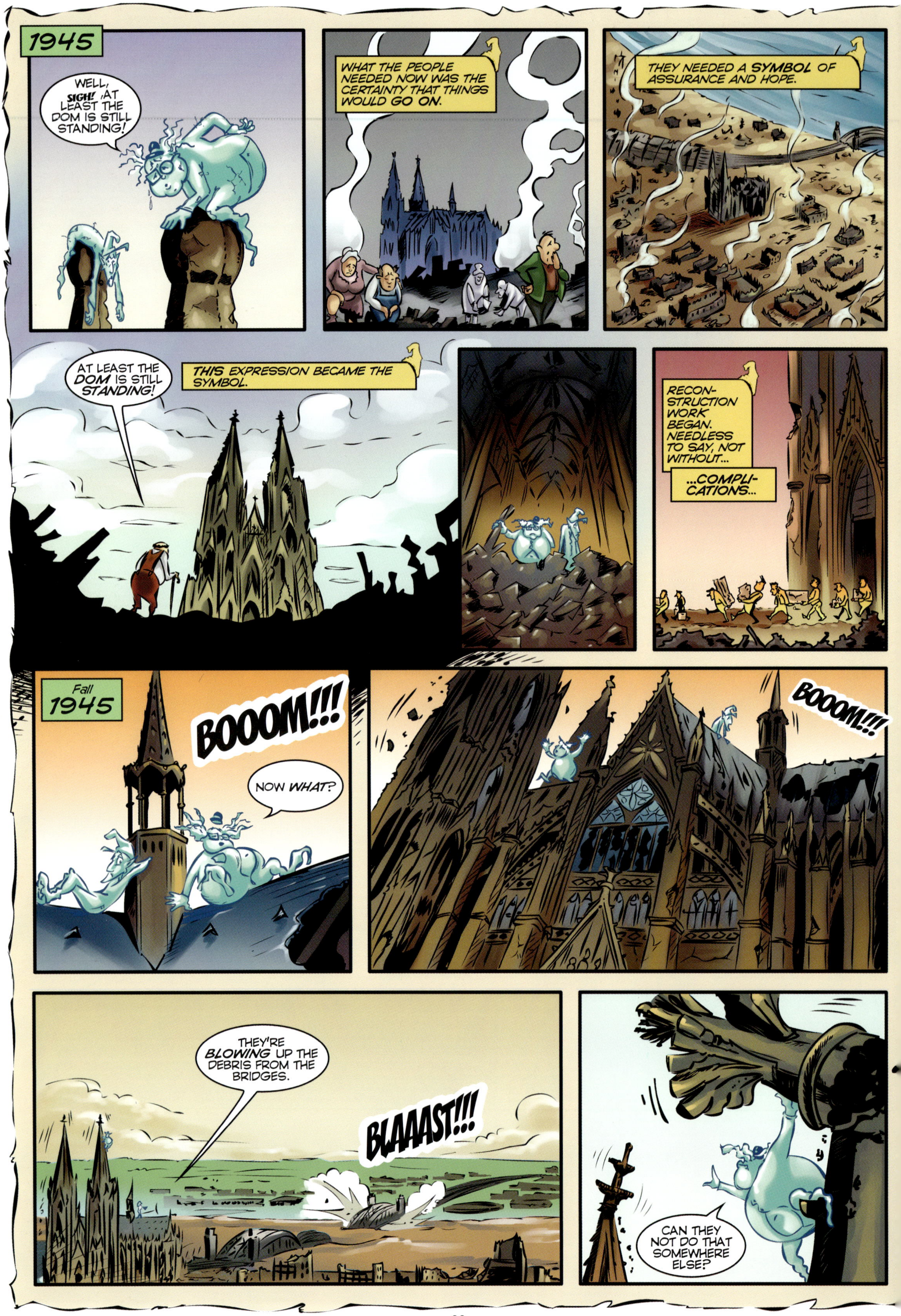
1945
WELL, SIGH! AT LEAST THE DOM IS STILL STANDING!
WHAT THE PEOPLE NEEDED NOW WAS THE CERTAINTY THAT THINGS WOULD GO ON.
THEY NEEDED A SYMBOL OF ASSURANCE AND HOPE.
AT LEAST THE DOM IS STILL STANDING!
THIS EXPRESSION BECAME THE SYMBOL.
RECONSTRUCTION WORK BEGAN. NEEDLESS TO SAY, NOT WITHOUT...
...COMPLICATIONS...
Fall 1945
BOOOM!!!
NOW WHAT?
BOOOM!!!
THEY'RE BLOWING UP THE DEBRIS FROM THE BRIDGES.
BLAAAST!!!
CAN THEY NOT DO THAT SOMEWHERE ELSE?

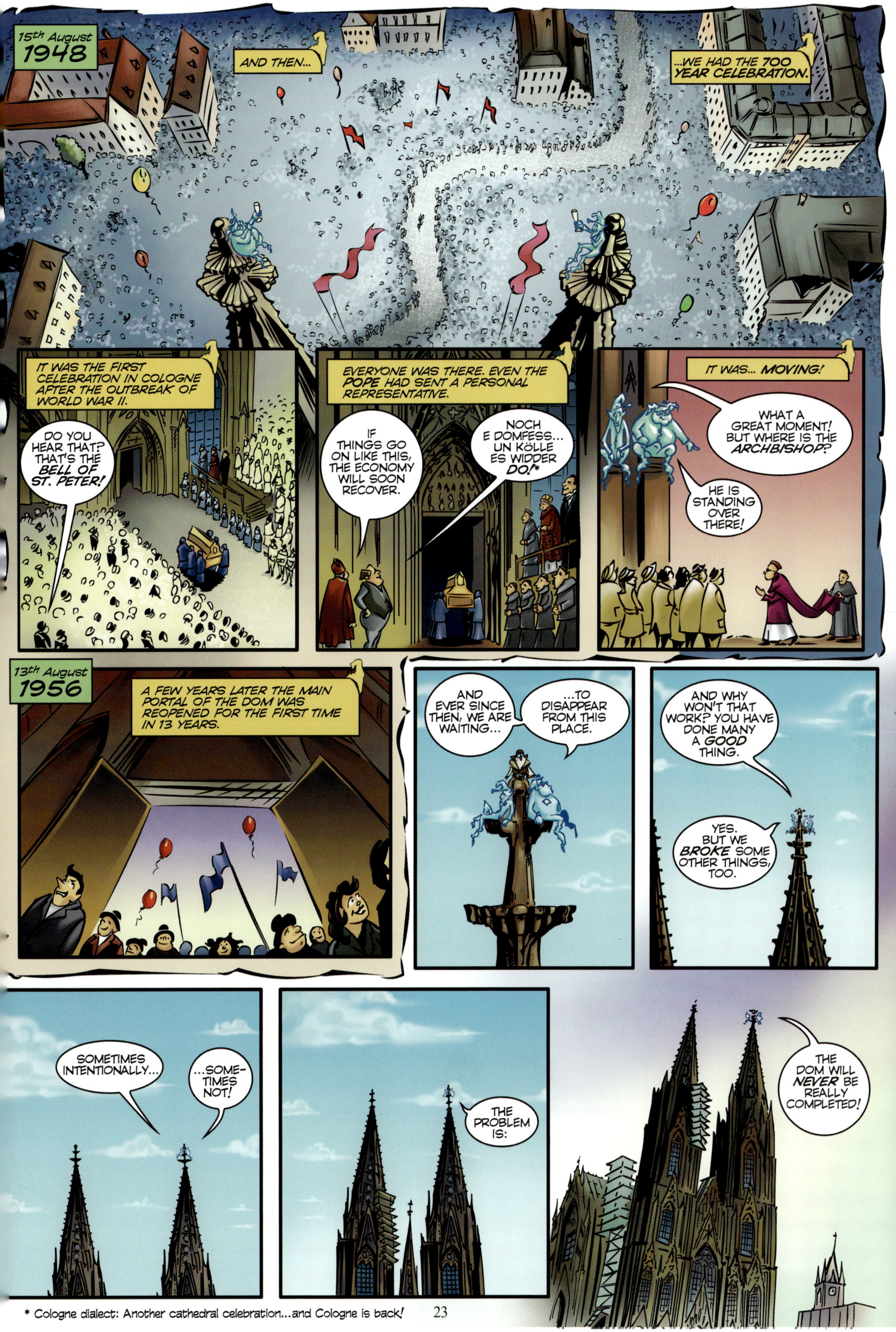
15th August 1948
AND THEN...
...WE HAD THE 700 YEAR CELEBRATION.
IT WAS THE FIRST CELEBRATION IN COLOGNE AFTER THE OUTBREAK OF WORLD WAR II.
DO YOU HEAR THAT? THAT'S THE BELL OF ST. PETER!
EVERYONE WAS THERE. EVEN THE POPE HAD SENT A PERSONAL REPRESENTATIVE.
IF THINGS GO ON LIKE THIS, THE ECONOMY WILL SOON RECOVER.
NOCH E DOMFESS... UN KÖLLE ES WIDDER DO!*
IT WAS... MOVING!
WHAT A GREAT MOMENT! BUT WHERE IS THE ARCHBISHOP?
HE IS STANDING OVER THERE!
13th August 1956
A FEW YEARS LATER THE MAIN PORTAL OF THE DOM WAS REOPENED FOR THE FIRST TIME IN 13 YEARS.
AND EVER SINCE THEN, WE ARE WAITING...
...TO DISAPPEAR FROM THIS PLACE.
AND WHY WON'T THAT WORK? YOU HAVE DONE MANY A GOOD THING.
YES. BUT WE BROKE SOME OTHER THINGS, TOO.
SOMETIMES INTENTIONALLY...
...SOME-TIMES NOT!
THE PROBLEM IS:
THE DOM WILL NEVER BE REALLY COMPLETED!

* Cologne dialect: Another cathedral celebration...and Cologne is back!

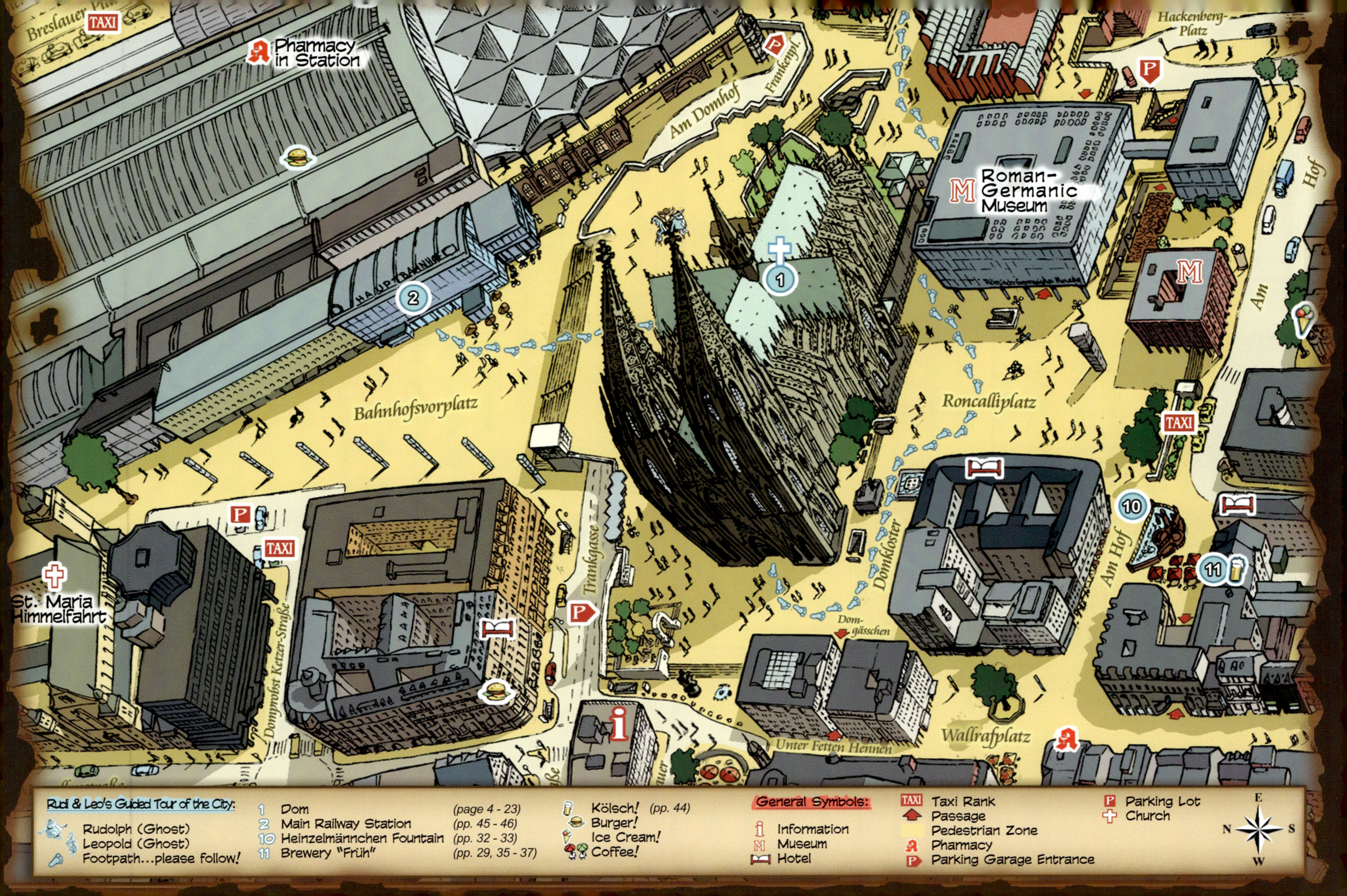
Breslauer Platz
TAXI
Pharmacy in Station
Am Domhof
Frankenpl.
Hackenberg-Platz
Roman-Germanic Museum
2
1
Bahnhofsvorplatz
Roncalliplatz
TAXI
10
11
Am Hof
Am
Hof
TAXI
St. Maria Himmelfahrt
Dompropst Ketzer-Straße
Trankgasse
Domkloster
Dom-gässchen
Unter Fetten Hennen
Wallrafplatz
Rudi & Leo's Guided Tour of the City:
Rudolph (Ghost)
Leopold (Ghost)
Footpath...please follow!
1 Dom (page 4 - 23)
2 Main Railway Station (pp. 45 - 46)
10 Heinzelmännchen Fountain (pp. 32 - 33)
11 Brewery "Früh" (pp. 29, 35 - 37)
Kölsch! (pp. 44)
Burger!
Ice Cream!
Coffee!
General Symbols:
Information
Museum
Hotel
Taxi Rank
Passage
Pedestrian Zone
Pharmacy
Parking Garage Entrance
Parking Lot
Church
N
E
S
W

WHAT BRINGS YOU TO COLOGNE ANYHOW?
THE SCOTTISH PRINCE FROM THE TRIUMVIRATE.* HIS NAME IS McGUFFIN ...
...AND HE'S SUPPOSED TO BE IN TOWN RIGHT NOW.
WE COULD HELP YOU FIND HIM!
Römisch-Germanisc
Museum
HELLO, WALTER.
HI GUYS!
WE ARE LOOKING FOR THE PRINCE FROM THE TRIUMVIRATE. A SCOTSMAN. HE'S SUPPOSED TO BE IN TOWN TODAY AND WE HAVE AN IMPORTANT MESSAGE FOR HIM.
I SEE.
I HEARD HE WENT DOWN TO THE RHINE.
LOOK, HOW CUTE. THE DOGGIE. TAKE A PICTURE DADDY!
WOOF WOOFIDDY WOOF!
WOOF-WOOF?
OH THAT'S SO CUTE.
WHO'S THE DOG TALKING TO?
HE IS TALKING TO THE AIR, THAT'S SO COOL!
CLICK!
I THINK HE'S TALKING TO THE PIGEON.
THANKS FOR THE HELP.
POLIZEI
TOURISTS!

* The Triumvirate in Cologne reigns during Karneval. It consists of the Prince, the Peasant and the Maiden.

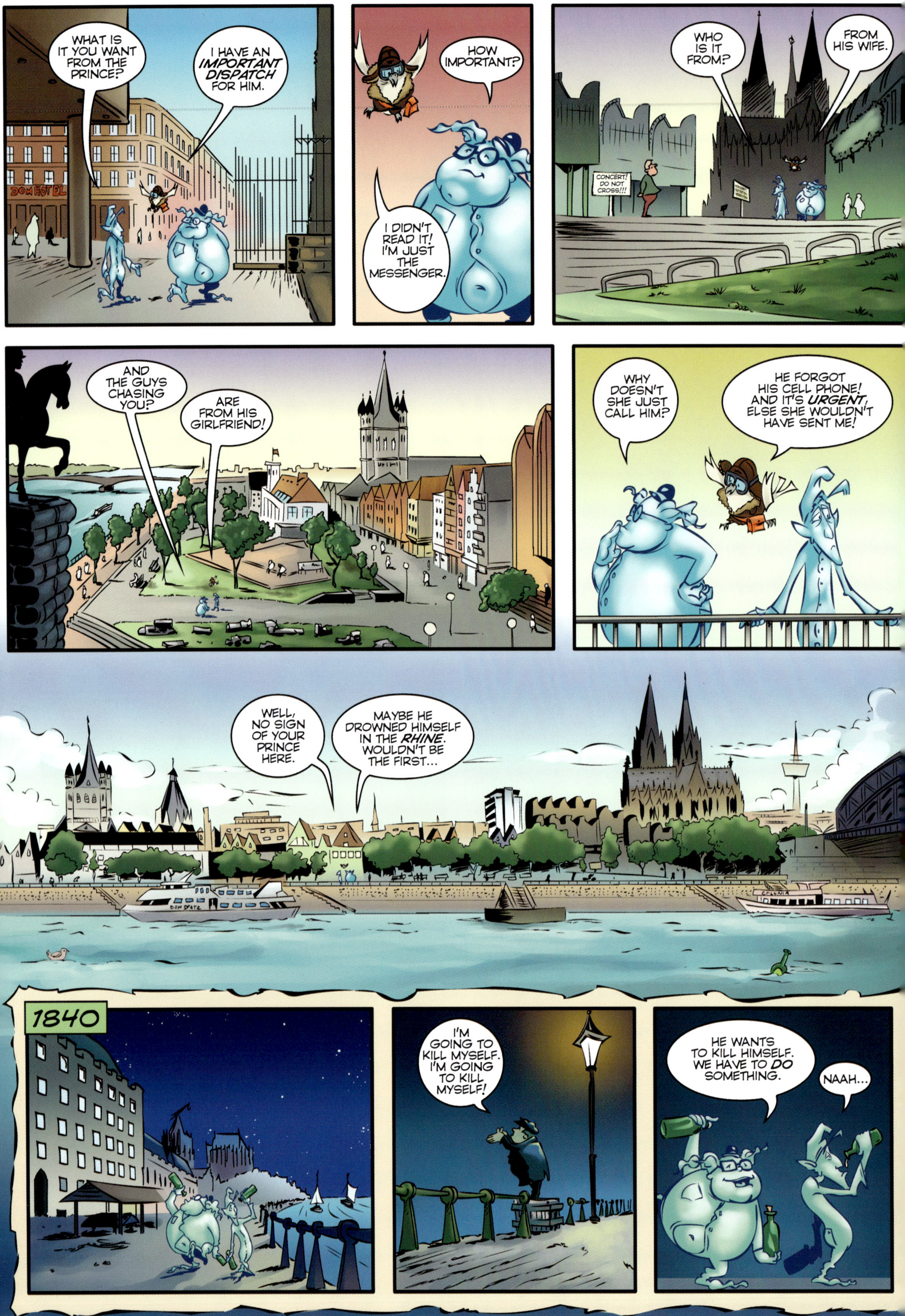

WHAT IS IT YOU WANT FROM THE PRINCE?
I HAVE AN IMPORTANT DISPATCH FOR HIM.
DOM HOTEL
HOW IMPORTANT?
I DIDN'T READ IT! I'M JUST THE MESSENGER.
WHO IS IT FROM?
FROM HIS WIFE.
CONCERT! DO NOT CROSS!!!
AND THE GUYS CHASING YOU?
ARE FROM HIS GIRLFRIEND!
WHY DOESN'T SHE JUST CALL HIM?
HE FORGOT HIS CELL PHONE! AND IT'S URGENT, ELSE SHE WOULDN'T HAVE SENT ME!
WELL, NO SIGN OF YOUR PRINCE HERE.
MAYBE HE DROWNED HIMSELF IN THE RHINE. WOULDN'T BE THE FIRST...
1840
I'M GOING TO KILL MYSELF. I'M GOING TO KILL MYSELF!
HE WANTS TO KILL HIMSELF. WE HAVE TO DO SOMETHING.
NAAH...

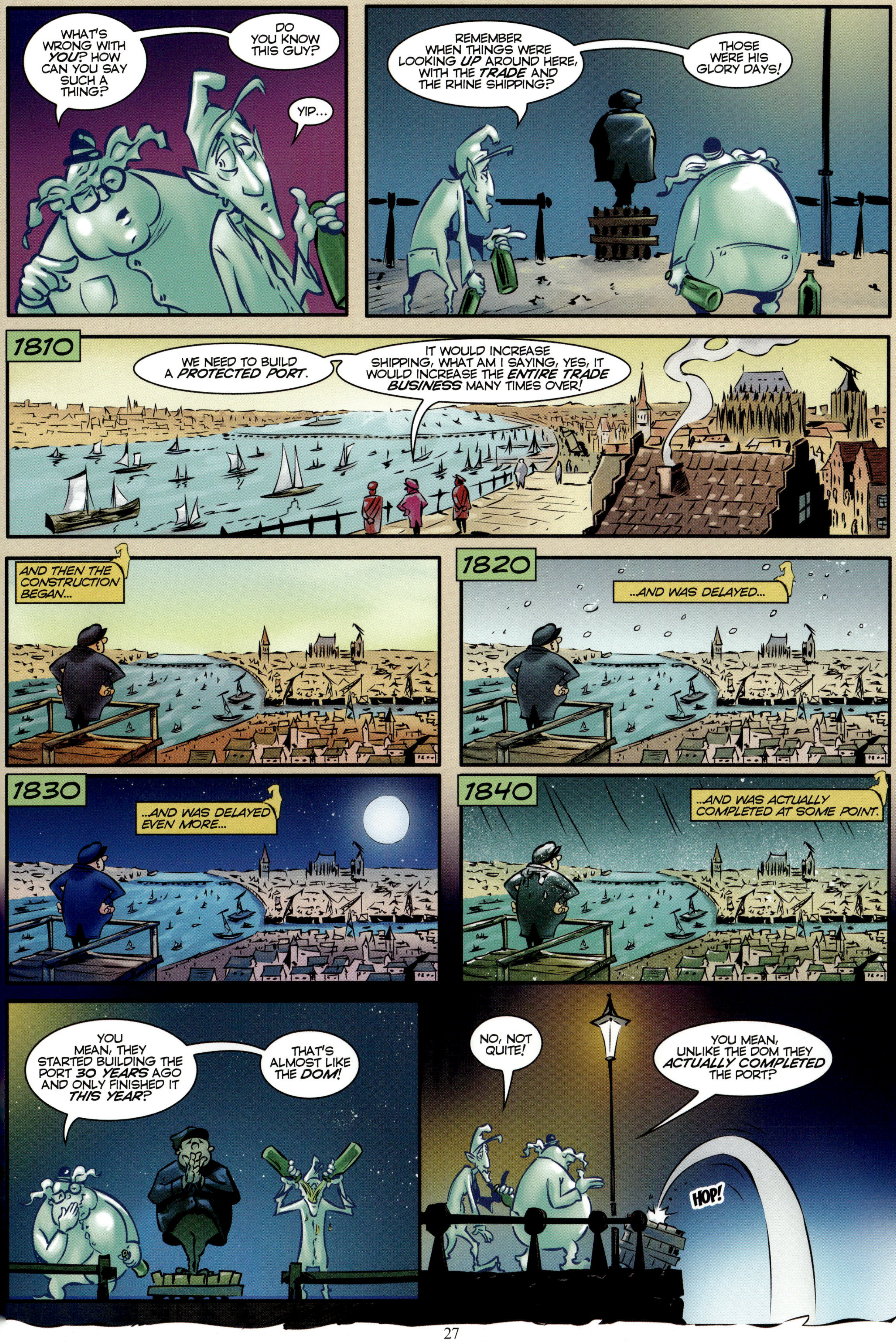
WHAT'S WRONG WITH YOU? HOW CAN YOU SAY SUCH A THING?
DO YOU KNOW THIS GUY?
YIP...
REMEMBER WHEN THINGS WERE LOOKING UP AROUND HERE, WITH THE TRADE AND THE RHINE SHIPPING?
THOSE WERE HIS GLORY DAYS!
1810
WE NEED TO BUILD A PROTECTED PORT.
IT WOULD INCREASE SHIPPING, WHAT AM I SAYING, YES, IT WOULD INCREASE THE ENTIRE TRADE BUSINESS MANY TIMES OVER!
AND THEN THE CONSTRUCTION BEGAN...
1820
...AND WAS DELAYED...
1830
...AND WAS DELAYED EVEN MORE...
1840
...AND WAS ACTUALLY COMPLETED AT SOME POINT.
YOU MEAN, THEY STARTED BUILDING THE PORT 30 YEARS AGO AND ONLY FINISHED IT THIS YEAR?
THAT'S ALMOST LIKE THE DOM!
NO, NOT QUITE!
YOU MEAN, UNLIKE THE DOM THEY ACTUALLY COMPLETED THE PORT?
HOP!

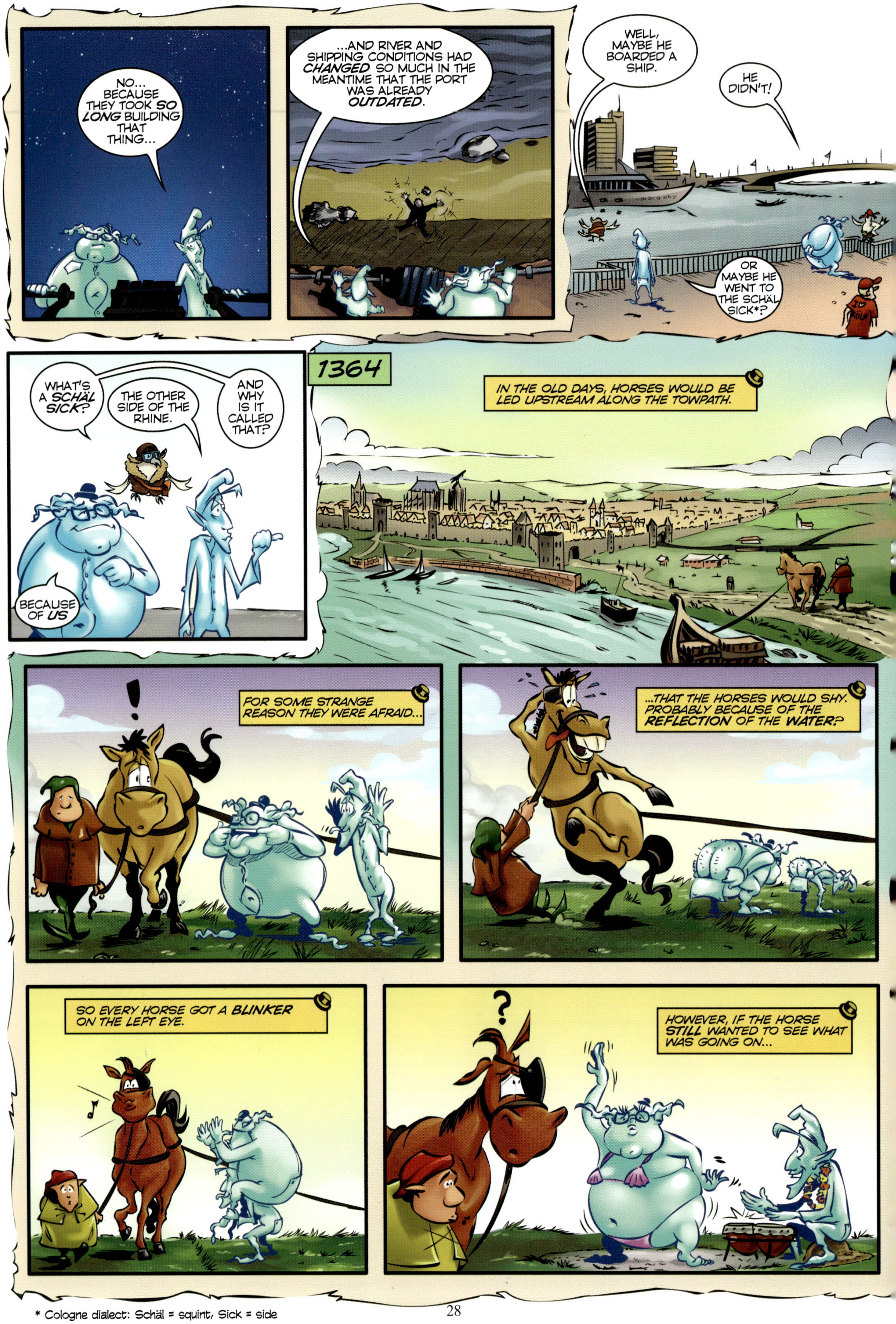
NO... BECAUSE THEY TOOK SO LONG BUILDING THAT THING...
...AND RIVER AND SHIPPING CONDITIONS HAD CHANGED SO MUCH IN THE MEANTIME THAT THE PORT WAS ALREADY OUTDATED.
WELL, MAYBE HE BOARDED A SHIP.
HE DIDN'T!
OR MAYBE HE WENT TO THE SCHÄL SICK*?
WHAT'S A SCHÄL SICK?
THE OTHER SIDE OF THE RHINE.
AND WHY IS IT CALLED THAT?
BECAUSE OF US
1364
IN THE OLD DAYS, HORSES WOULD BE LED UPSTREAM ALONG THE TOWPATH.
FOR SOME STRANGE REASON THEY WERE AFRAID...
!
...THAT THE HORSES WOULD SHY. PROBABLY BECAUSE OF THE REFLECTION OF THE WATER?
SO EVERY HORSE GOT A BLINKER ON THE LEFT EYE.
?
HOWEVER, IF THE HORSE STILL WANTED TO SEE WHAT WAS GOING ON...

* Cologne dialect: Schäl = squint, Sick = side

...IT HAD TO SQUINT OVER ITS BLINKER.
?
THIS IS BORING!
HENCE THE TERM "SCHÄL SICK", FROM SQUINTING.
BUT IN COLOGNE DIALECT IT ALSO REFERS TO SOMETHING "BAD" OR "WRONG", WHICH ALSO FITS WELL!
AND WHAT ABOUT THE PRINCE?
SOMEONE HEARD THAT HE WANTED TO GO TO GROSS ST. MARTIN'S CHURCH.
GROSS ST. MARTIN!
THERE WAS THIS FANTASTIC STORY...
1378
?
RRRRRIP!!!
...OH NO THERE WASN'T!
?!
?
Nº11

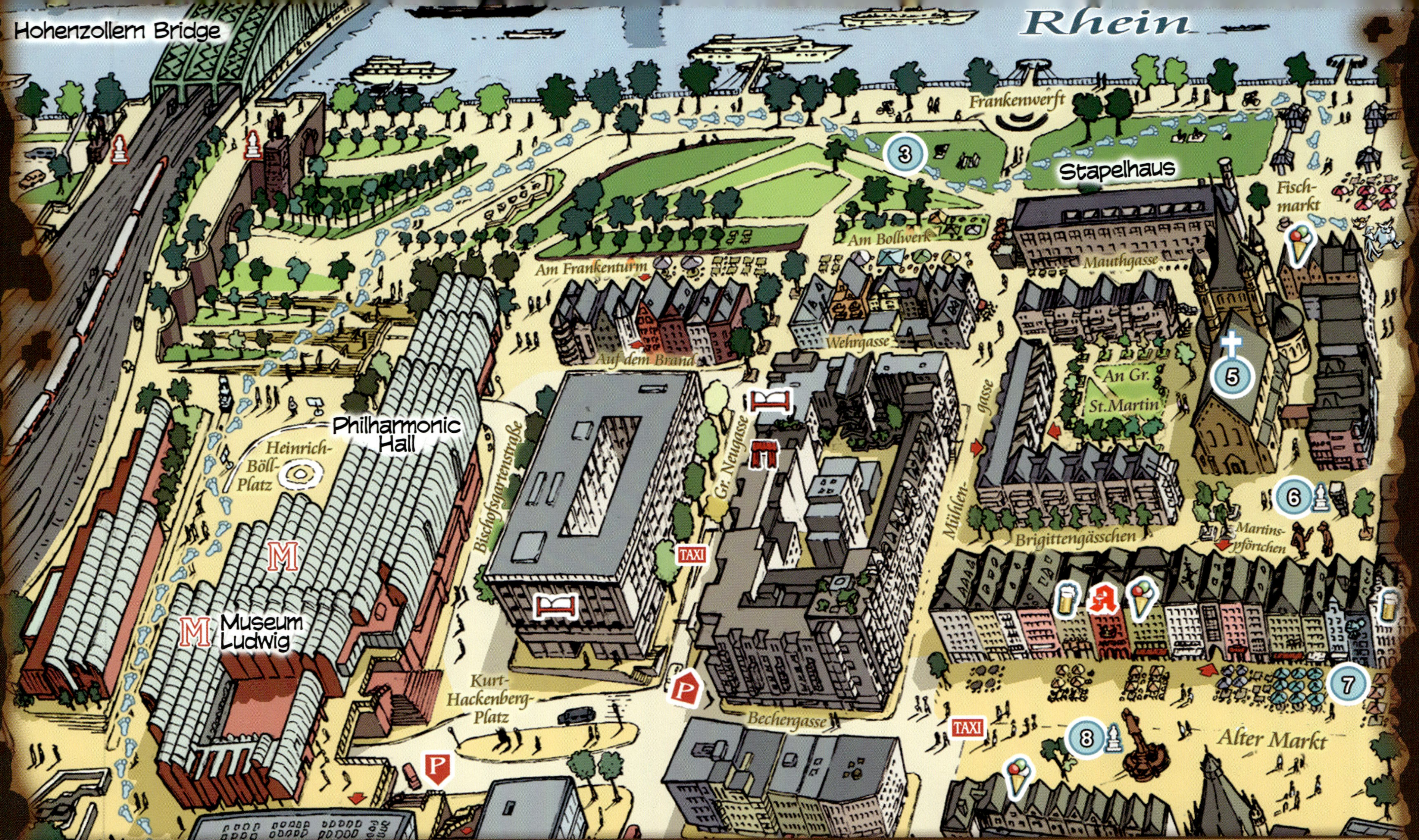

Rudi & Leo's Guided Tour of the City:

Rudolph (Ghost)
Leopold (Ghost)
Footpath...please follow!

3 Rheingarten (page 26 - 29)
5 Groß St. Martin (pp. 29, 35 - 37)
6 Tünnes and Schäl (pp. 31 - 33)
7 Kallendresser (pp. 35 - 38)
8 Jan v. Werth Brunnen (pp. 39 - 40)

Kölsch! (pp. 44)
Ice Cream!
Coffee!

General Symbols:

Museum
Monument
Theater
Hotel
Taxi Rank
Passage
Pedestrian Zone
Pharmacy
Parking Garage Entrance
Church

N E S W

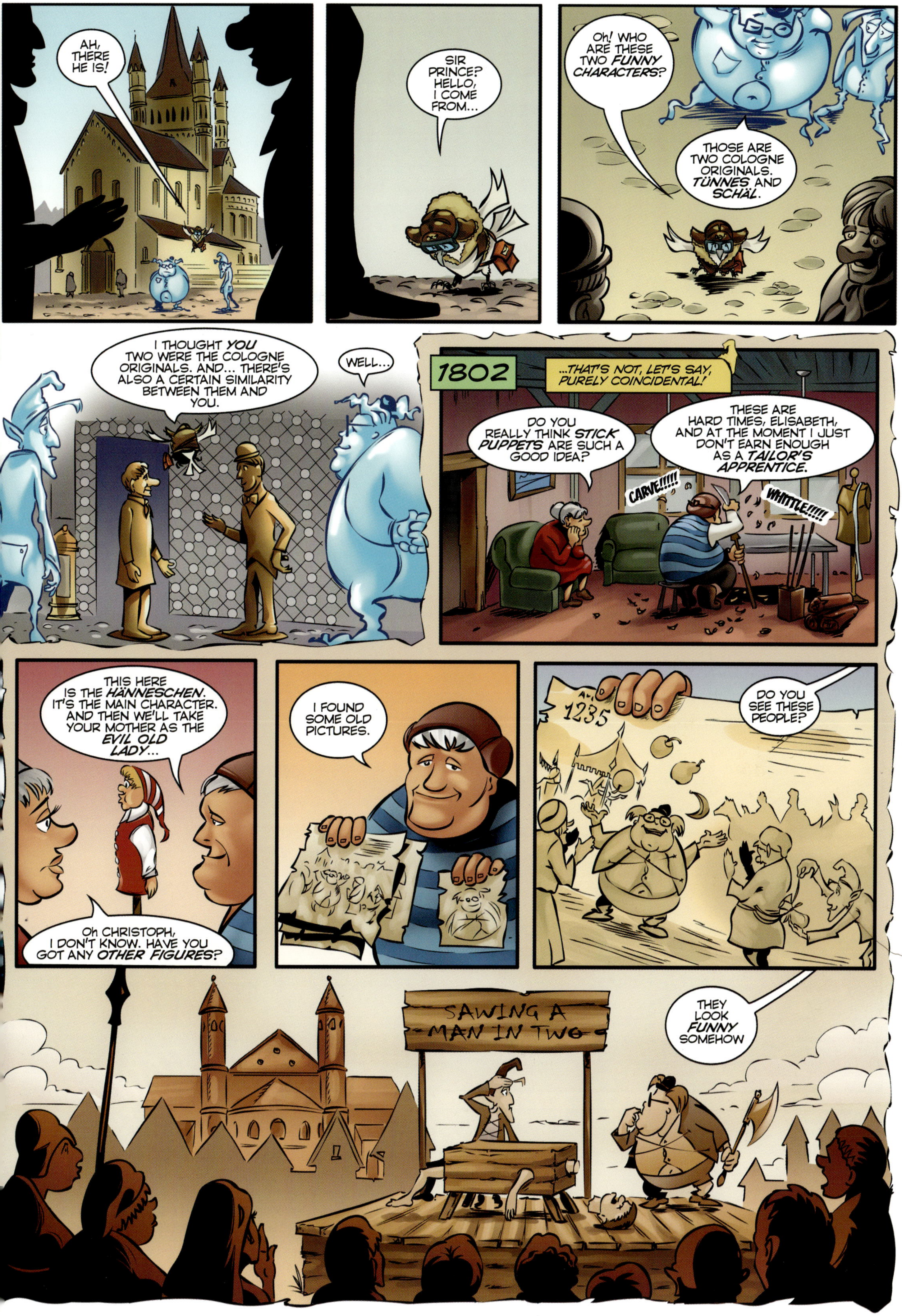
AH, THERE HE IS!
SIR PRINCE? HELLO, I COME FROM...
Oh! WHO ARE THESE TWO FUNNY CHARACTERS?
THOSE ARE TWO COLOGNE ORIGINALS. TÜNNES AND SCHÄL.
I THOUGHT YOU TWO WERE THE COLOGNE ORIGINALS. AND... THERE'S ALSO A CERTAIN SIMILARITY BETWEEN THEM AND YOU.
WELL...
1802
...THAT'S NOT, LET'S SAY, PURELY COINCIDENTAL!
DO YOU REALLY THINK STICK PUPPETS ARE SUCH A GOOD IDEA?
THESE ARE HARD TIMES, ELISABETH, AND AT THE MOMENT I JUST DON'T EARN ENOUGH AS A TAILOR'S APPRENTICE.
CARVE!!!!!
WHITTLE!!!!!
THIS HERE IS THE HÄNNESCHEN. IT'S THE MAIN CHARACTER. AND THEN WE'LL TAKE YOUR MOTHER AS THE EVIL OLD LADY...
Oh CHRISTOPH, I DON'T KNOW. HAVE YOU GOT ANY OTHER FIGURES?
I FOUND SOME OLD PICTURES.
1235
DO YOU SEE THESE PEOPLE?
SAWING A MAN IN TWO
THEY LOOK FUNNY SOMEHOW

SOMEHOW...
- yawn - I'LL DO SOMETHING WITH YOU, I'M JUST NOT SURE WHAT - yawn -
YET...
SNORE!
YOU KNOW WHAT I DON'T UNDERSTAND? WOMEN!
A NICE HANDKERCHIEF, A HANDBAG, A HANDSHAKE...
...BUT IF YOU DO BRING SOMETHING HOME TO HER...
Opening Today.
Hänneschen Theater
...YOU JUST CAN'T SEEM TO GET IT RIGHT!
AND WHAT DID YOU BRING HER?
A HANGOVER!
Hänneschen Theater
AND WHAT DID YOU BRING HER, TÜNNES?
A HANGOVER!
HAHA!
HAHA! HAHAHA!
HAHA! HAHAHA!

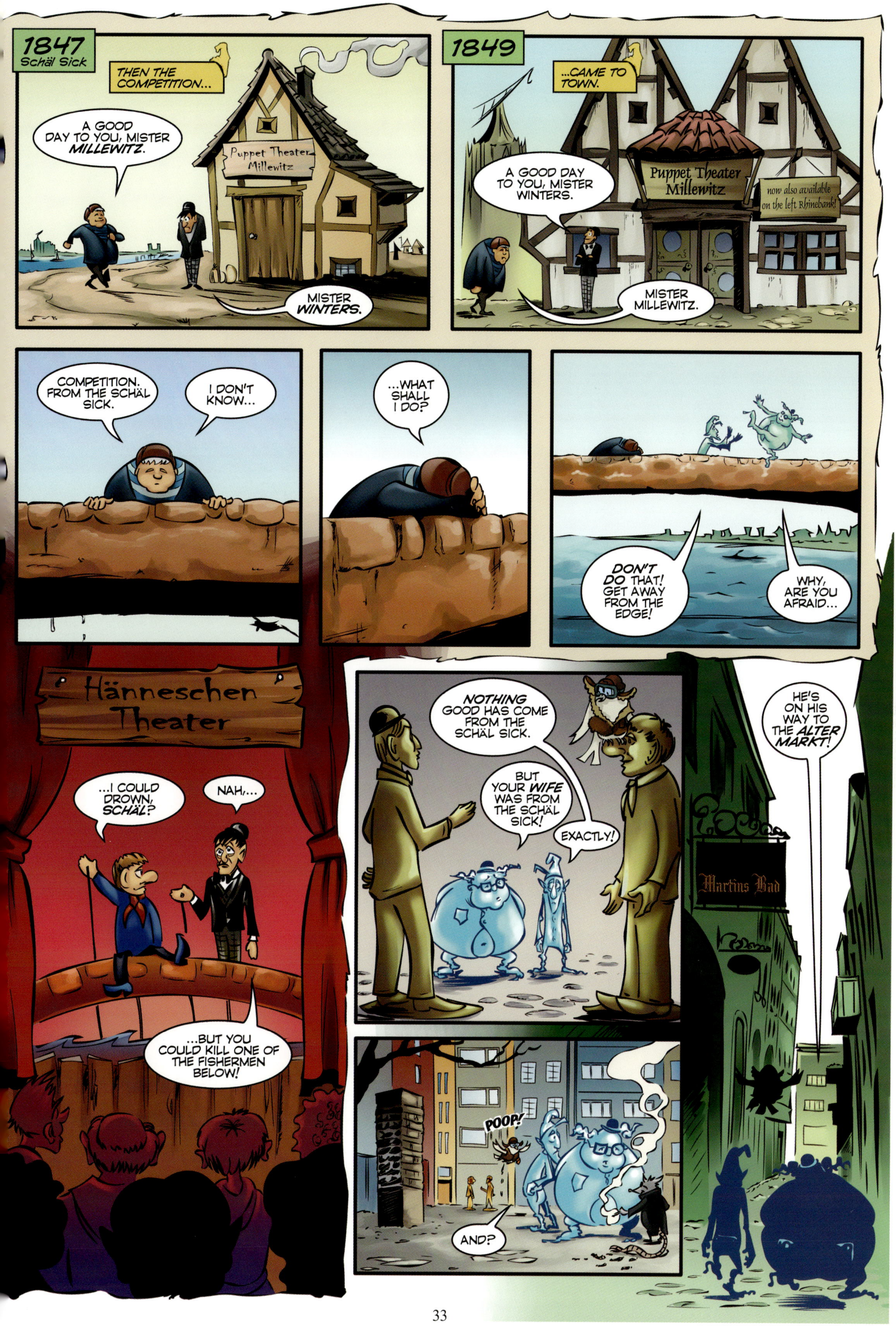
1847
Schäl Sick
THEN THE COMPETITION...
Puppet Theater Millewitz
A GOOD DAY TO YOU, MISTER MILLEWITZ.
MISTER WINTERS.
1849
...CAME TO TOWN.
Puppet Theater Millewitz
now also available on the left Rhinebank!
A GOOD DAY TO YOU, MISTER WINTERS.
MISTER MILLEWITZ.
COMPETITION. FROM THE SCHÄL SICK.
I DON'T KNOW...
...WHAT SHALL I DO?
DON'T DO THAT! GET AWAY FROM THE EDGE!
WHY, ARE YOU AFRAID...
Hänneschen Theater
...I COULD DROWN, SCHÄL?
NAH,...
...BUT YOU COULD KILL ONE OF THE FISHERMEN BELOW!
NOTHING GOOD HAS COME FROM THE SCHÄL SICK.
BUT YOUR WIFE WAS FROM THE SCHÄL SICK!
EXACTLY!
Martins Bad
HE'S ON HIS WAY TO THE ALTER MARKT!
POOP!
AND?

Frankenwerft
Stapelhaus
Fisch-
markt
Am Bollwerk
Mauthgasse
Wehrgasse
An Gr.
St.Martin
Gr. Neugasse
Mühlen-
gasse
Brigittengässchen
Martins-
pförtchen
Butter-
markt
Hafengasse
Rote-
Funken-
Pl.
Auf dem
Rothenberg
Salzgasse
Lintgasse
Kastellg.
Ostermann-
platz
Eisen-
markt
Markmannsgasse
Halb-
mondg.
Faßbinderg.
Heumarkt
Unter
Käster
Alter Markt
Bechergasse
Unter Taschenmacher
Hühner-
gasse
Seidenmacherinnengässchen
City Hall
TAXI
Rudi & Leo's Guided Tour of the City:
Rudolph (Ghost)
Leopold (Ghost)
Footpath...please follow!
3 Rheingarten (page 26 - 29)
4 Hänneschen Theater (pp. 32 - 33)
5 Groß St. Martin (pp. 29, 35 - 37)
6 Tünnes and Schäl (pp. 31 - 33)
7 Kallendresser (pp. 39 - 40)
8 Jan v. Werth Fountain (pp. 39 - 40)
Kölsch! (pp. 44)
Ice Cream!
Coffee!
General Symbols:
Museum
Monument
Theater
Hotel
Taxi Rank
Passage
Pedestrian Zone
Pharmacy
Church
E
N
S
W

WHAT IS THAT?
THAT'S THE KALLEN-DRESSER.*
WHAT'S... HE DOING?
WELL, WHAT DO YOU THINK PIGEONS LIKE TO DO BEST?
POOP ON PEOPLE'S HEADS?
EXACTLY. AND THAT'S WHAT HE IS DOING...
BUT INTO THE EAVES GUTTER.
AND WHY DID HE RECEIVE A MONUMENT LIKE THIS ONE?
Ah WELL, RUDI AND I DON'T AGREE ON THIS ONE.
IF YOU ASK ME, THE STORY ABOUT THE KALLENDRESSER HAPPENED...
...AS FOLLOWS...
1600 CHURCH OF GROSS ST. MARTIN...
THERE WAS THIS CULPRIT...
Hey RUDI, QUIT IT!
Burp!
The Great St. Martin
YOU FIND HIM SUCH A BORE
THE MAN WHO SHARED ALL HE CAN
IN BIG AND SMALL AND RICH AND POOR
ST. MARTIN WAS A REAL GREAT MAN!
Rudi
...WHO TOOK REFUGE IN THE PROTECTION OF GROSS ST. MARTIN...
YOU WILL NEVER BE A POET!
Gulp!

* "Dä Kallendresser", on house No. 24 on Alter Markt. The figure was created by Ewald Mataré. However, his intellectual father was Jupp Engels (1909-1991) who liked to call himself the "Oberkallendresser" in his lifetime. "Kall" is Cologne dialect for an eaves gutter.

THE COLOGNE CITIZENS WEREN'T HAPPY ABOUT THE WAY...
...THE ABBOT OF THE MONASTERY HAD DEALT WITH THE MATTER.
LEO?
WHY? WHAT DID THE ABBOT DO?
WELL, IT HAPPENED AS FOLLOWS...
LET'S MAKE SHADOW FIGURES!
GHOSTS DON'T HAVE A SHADOW!!!
EVEN ALTHOUGH THE CULPRIT SOUGHT PROTECTION IN THE CHURCH...
SIR ABBOT, PLEASE HELP ME!
A CULPRIT IS SUPPOSED TO BE HIDING HERE IN GROSS ST. MARTIN!
YOU KNOW THE POSITION OF THE CHURCH IN THIS!
UN-FORTUNATELY, I CANNOT HELP YOU!
BUT...ehm HE'S IN LEAGUE WITH THE DEVIL!
THE CULPRIT Hic! HAS A SHADOW!
...Oh YES Burp! SEEMS SOMEHOW...
...DEVILISH!
...THE ABBOT...
What?

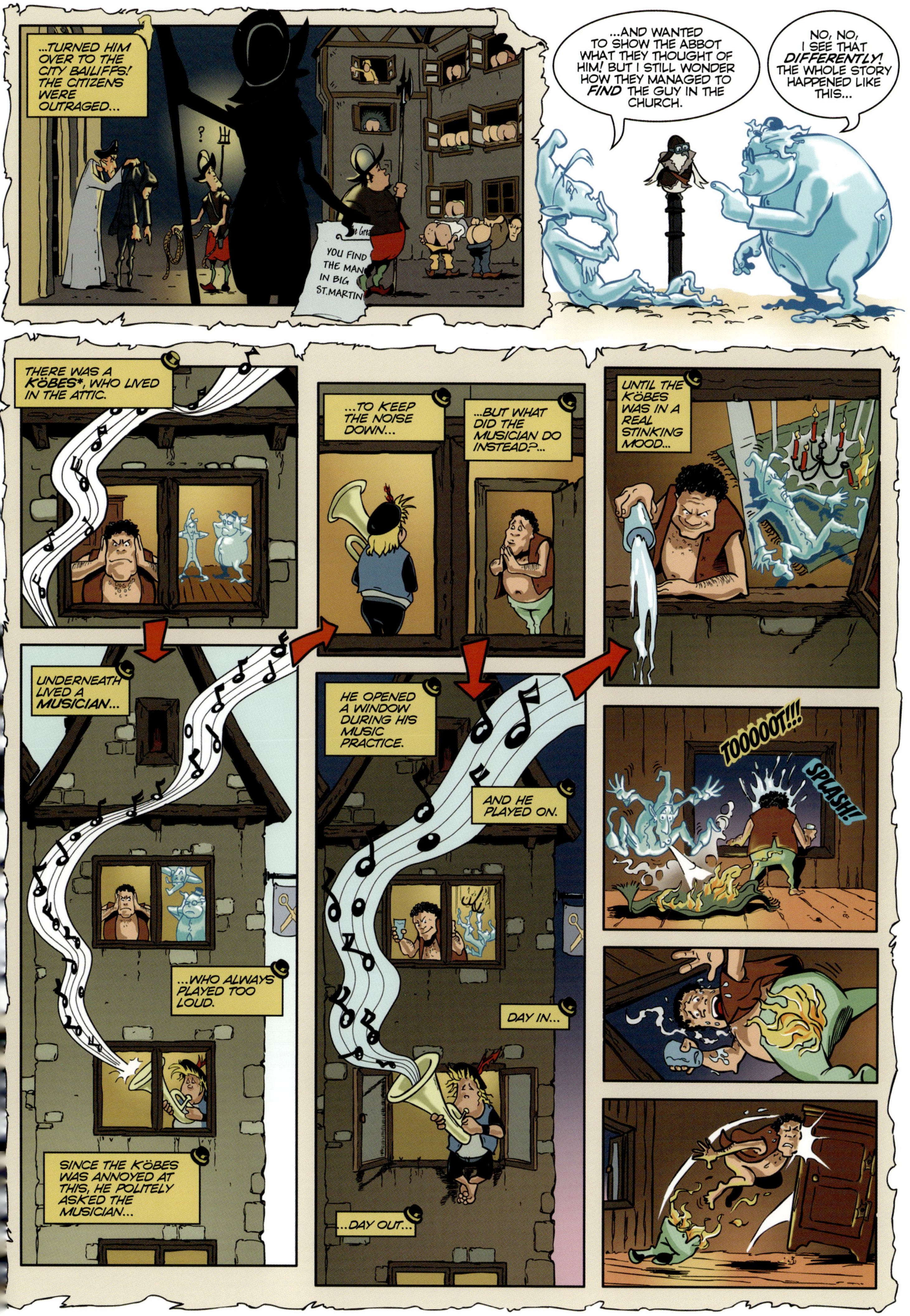

...TURNED HIM OVER TO THE CITY BAILIFFS! THE CITIZENS WERE OUTRAGED...
YOU FIND THE MAN IN BIG ST.MARTIN
...AND WANTED TO SHOW THE ABBOT WHAT THEY THOUGHT OF HIM! BUT I STILL WONDER HOW THEY MANAGED TO FIND THE GUY IN THE CHURCH.
NO, NO, I SEE THAT DIFFERENTLY! THE WHOLE STORY HAPPENED LIKE THIS...
THERE WAS A KÖBES*, WHO LIVED IN THE ATTIC.
UNDERNEATH LIVED A MUSICIAN...
...WHO ALWAYS PLAYED TOO LOUD.
SINCE THE KÖBES WAS ANNOYED AT THIS, HE POLITELY ASKED THE MUSICIAN...
...TO KEEP THE NOISE DOWN...
...BUT WHAT DID THE MUSICIAN DO INSTEAD?...
HE OPENED A WINDOW DURING HIS MUSIC PRACTICE.
AND HE PLAYED ON.
DAY IN...
...DAY OUT...
UNTIL THE KÖBES WAS IN A REAL STINKING MOOD...
TOOOOOT!!!
SPLASH!

* A traditional waiter in Cologne who serves Kölsch beer.

HOT! HOT! HOT!
GIVE HIM SOMETHING TO PUT THE FIRE OUT!
SLAAM!
GET ON WITH IT, LEO!
Phew...
...THAT WAS CLOSE!
SSSHHH!
Gulp! Gulp!
Castor Oil
Gulp! Gulp!
!?
Oh NO!
Ah, WHAT THE HELL!
AHHH!
...IN THE TRUEST SENSE OF THE WORD!
I SAY! PERHAPS THE ARTIST JUST WANTED TO SHOW THAT PEOPLE ON THE TOP FLOOR WERE OFTEN *TOO LAZY* TO GO TO THE TOILET IN THE YARD, SO THEY DID THEIR BUSINESS IN THE GUTTER!
Poop!

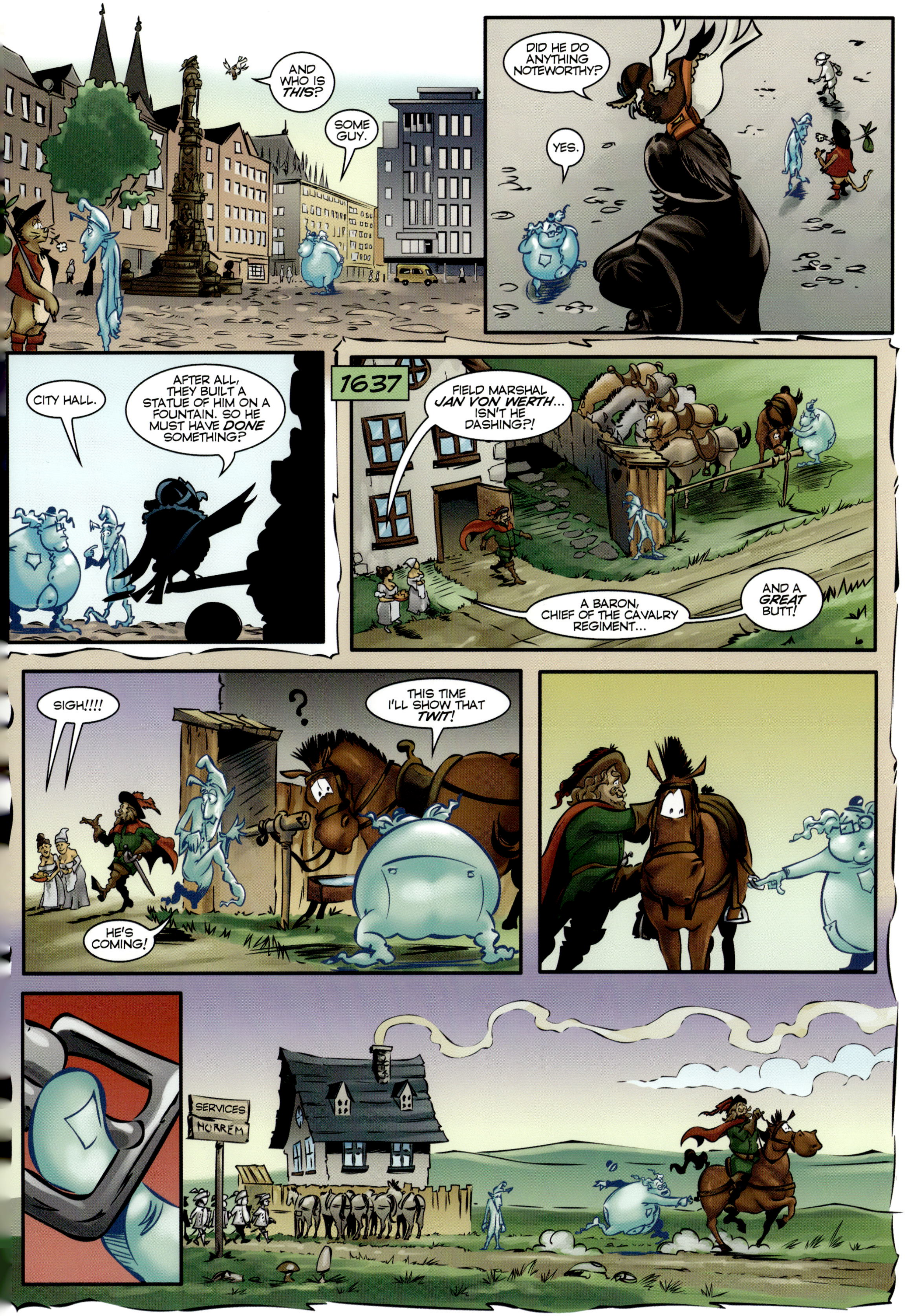
AND WHO IS THIS?
SOME GUY.
DID HE DO ANYTHING NOTEWORTHY?
YES.
CITY HALL.
AFTER ALL, THEY BUILT A STATUE OF HIM ON A FOUNTAIN. SO HE MUST HAVE DONE SOMETHING?
1637
FIELD MARSHAL JAN VON WERTH... ISN'T HE DASHING?!
A BARON, CHIEF OF THE CAVALRY REGIMENT...
AND A GREAT BUTT!
SIGH!!!!
?
THIS TIME I'LL SHOW THAT TWIT!
HE'S COMING!
SERVICES
HÜRREM

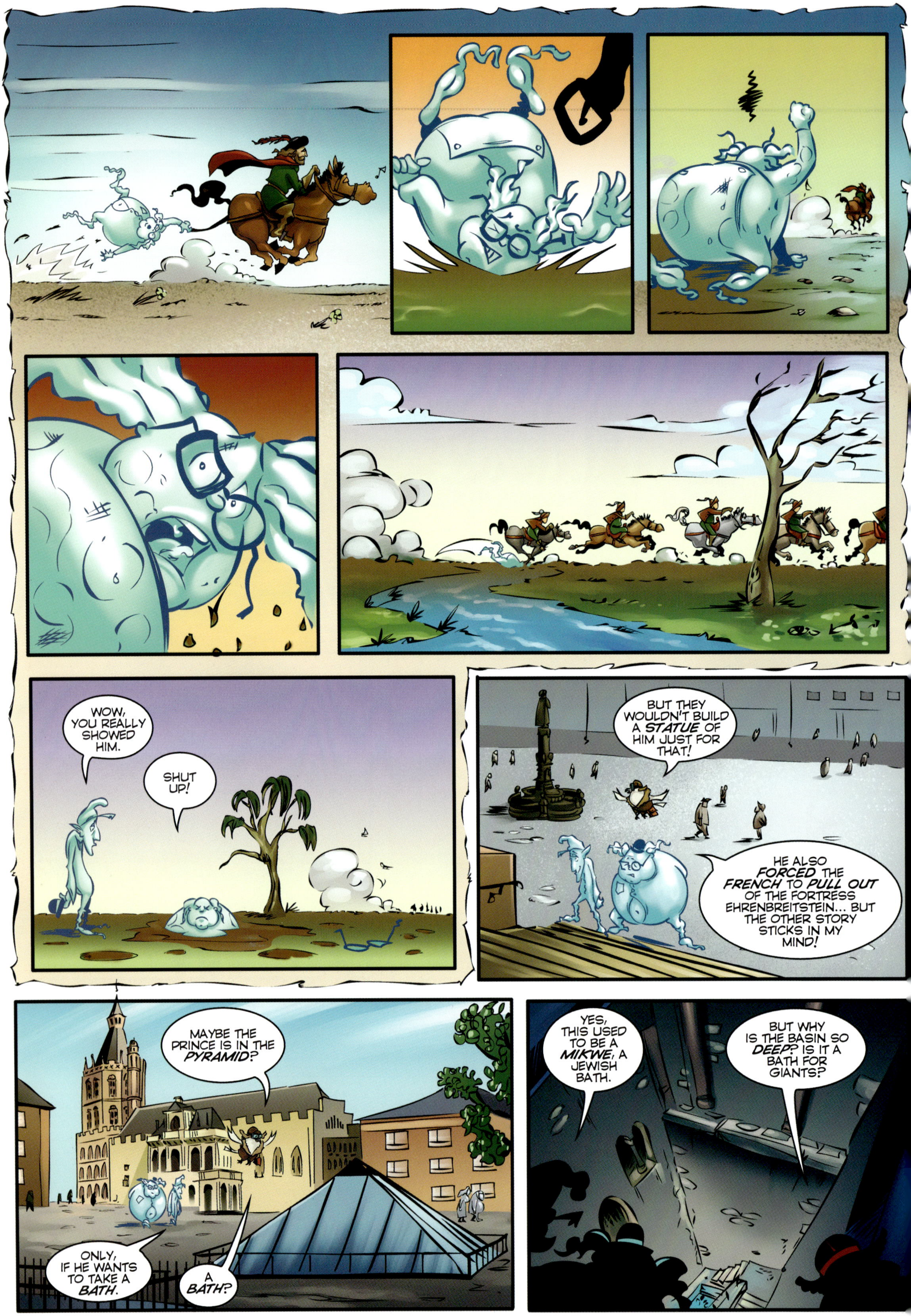
WOW, YOU REALLY SHOWED HIM.
SHUT UP!
BUT THEY WOULDN'T BUILD A STATUE OF HIM JUST FOR THAT!
HE ALSO FORCED THE FRENCH TO PULL OUT OF THE FORTRESS EHRENBREITSTEIN... BUT THE OTHER STORY STICKS IN MY MIND!
MAYBE THE PRINCE IS IN THE PYRAMID?
ONLY, IF HE WANTS TO TAKE A BATH.
A BATH?
YES, THIS USED TO BE A MIKWE, A JEWISH BATH.
BUT WHY IS THE BASIN SO DEEP? IS IT A BATH FOR GIANTS?

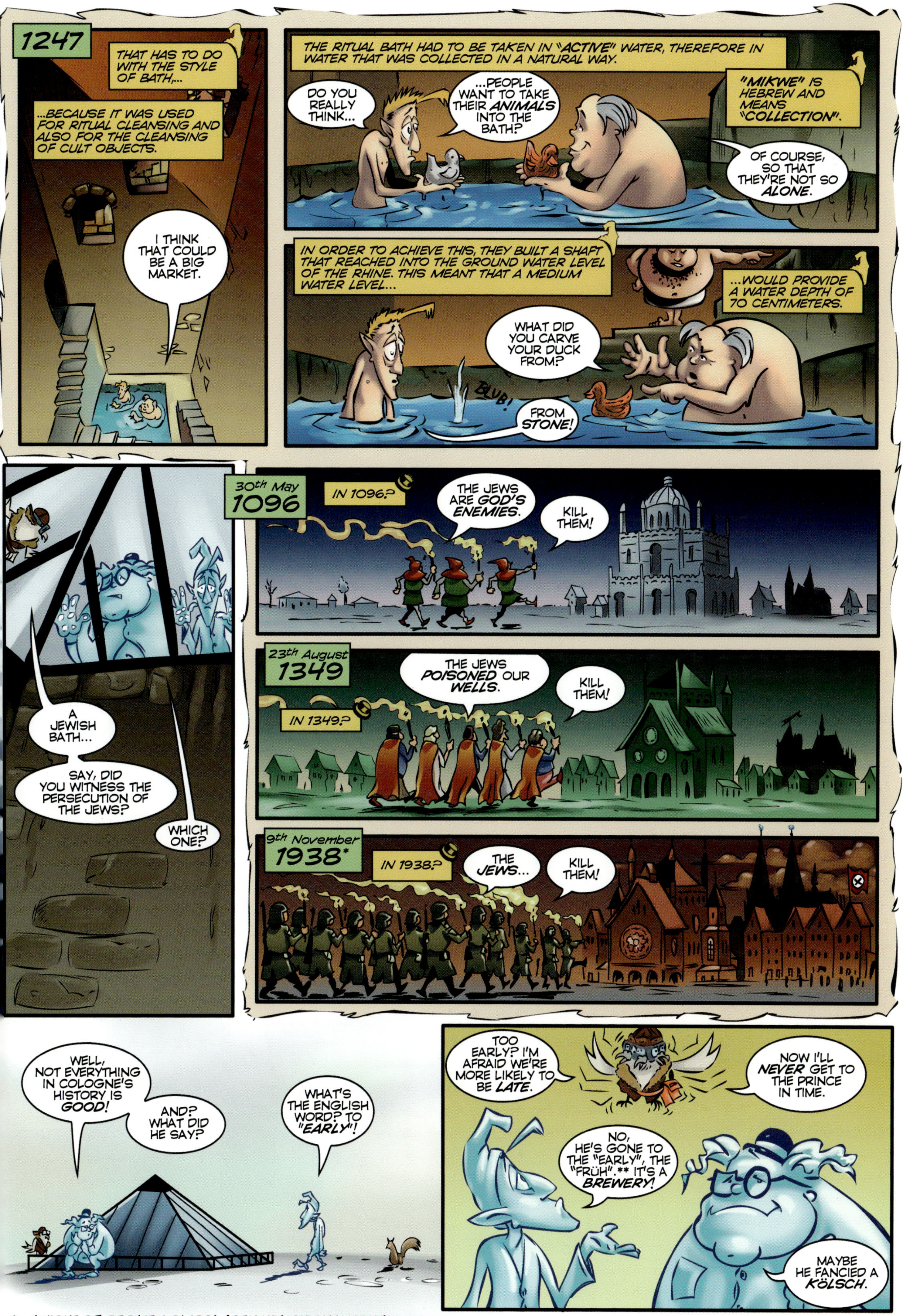
1247
THAT HAS TO DO WITH THE STYLE OF BATH,...
...BECAUSE IT WAS USED FOR RITUAL CLEANSING AND ALSO FOR THE CLEANSING OF CULT OBJECTS.
I THINK THAT COULD BE A BIG MARKET.
THE RITUAL BATH HAD TO BE TAKEN IN "ACTIVE" WATER, THEREFORE IN WATER THAT WAS COLLECTED IN A NATURAL WAY.
DO YOU REALLY THINK...
...PEOPLE WANT TO TAKE THEIR ANIMALS INTO THE BATH?
"MIKWE" IS HEBREW AND MEANS "COLLECTION".
OF COURSE, SO THAT THEY'RE NOT SO ALONE.
IN ORDER TO ACHIEVE THIS, THEY BUILT A SHAFT THAT REACHED INTO THE GROUND WATER LEVEL OF THE RHINE. THIS MEANT THAT A MEDIUM WATER LEVEL...
...WOULD PROVIDE A WATER DEPTH OF 70 CENTIMETERS.
WHAT DID YOU CARVE YOUR DUCK FROM?
BLUB!
FROM STONE!
A JEWISH BATH...
SAY, DID YOU WITNESS THE PERSECUTION OF THE JEWS?
WHICH ONE?
30th May 1096
IN 1096?
THE JEWS ARE GOD'S ENEMIES.
KILL THEM!
23th August 1349
THE JEWS POISONED OUR WELLS.
KILL THEM!
IN 1349?
9th November 1938*
IN 1938?
THE JEWS...
KILL THEM!
WELL, NOT EVERYTHING IN COLOGNE'S HISTORY IS GOOD!
AND? WHAT DID HE SAY?
WHAT'S THE ENGLISH WORD? TO "EARLY"!
TOO EARLY? I'M AFRAID WE'RE MORE LIKELY TO BE LATE.
NOW I'LL NEVER GET TO THE PRINCE IN TIME.
NO, HE'S GONE TO THE "EARLY", THE "FRÜH".** IT'S A BREWERY!
MAYBE HE FANCIED A KÖLSCH.

* "NIGHT OF BROKEN GLASS" (REICHSKRISTALLNACHT)

** Früh = German for 'early')

Roman-Germanic Museum
Am Hof
Alter Markt
Unter Taschenmacher
Bürgerstraße
Praertorium
City Hall
City Hall
Rathaus-platz
Juden-gasse
Mars-platz
Steinweg
Martinstraße
Wallraf-Richartz-Museum
St. Alban
Gürzenich
Kleine Budengasse
Theo-Burauen-Platz
Unter Goldschmied
Große Budengasse
Sporer Gasse
Laurenzplatz
Salomons-gasse
Marspforten
Obenmarspforten
Große Sandkaul
Quatermarkt
In der
Hohe Straße
Hackenberg-Platz
Bechergasse
Unter
Kaster
Hühner-gasse
Gülichplatz
Portalsgasse
Schmitz-Platz
Minoritenstr.
Rudi & Leo's Guided Tour of the City:
Rudolph (Ghost)
Leopold (Ghost)
Footpath...please follow!
7 Kallendresser (page 35 - 38)
8 Jan v. Werth Fountain (pp. 39 - 40)
9 Mikwe (pp. 40 - 41)
10 Heinzelmännchen Fountain (pp. 43 - 44)
11 Brewery "Früh" (pp. 44 - 45)
Kölsch! (pp. 44)
Burger!
Ice Cream!
Coffee!
General Symbols:
Museum
Monument
Hotel
Taxi Rank
Passage
Pedestrian Zone
Pharmacy
Parking Garage Entrance
Parking Lot
Church
N
E
S
W

AH, FINALLY...
...WE FOUND THE PRINCE?
...WE'LL GET SOMETHING TO DRINK!
DON'T WORRY, THE PRINCE IS ALSO HERE. HE'S AT THE BAR AND KNOCKING DOWN THE KÖLSCH.
WHAT LUCK.
Phew, THAT WAS CLOSE.
NICE FOUNTAIN. DOES IT ALSO HAVE A STORY?
WE'RE IN COLOGNE, ALMOST EVERYTHING HAS A STORY. THAT'S THE HEINZELMÄNNCHEN-BRUNNEN...
1783
...CRAFTED BY EDMUND AND HEINRICH RENARD.
LEO, I'VE GOT AN IDEA!
I THINK THE PEOPLE ARE TOO BUSY WITH THINGS THAT KEEP THEM FROM DOING THE REAL IMPORTANT STUFF.
YOU MEAN, COMPLETING THE DOM.
PRECISELY!
THE COLOGNE BEAUTIFICATION ASSOCIATION DONATED IT IN 1899 ON THE OCCASION OF AUGUST KOPISCH'S HUNDREDTH BIRTHDAY.
Bakery
Butchery
SO WE DO ALL THEIR WORK FOR THEM...
HE WROTE A FAMOUS POEM ON THE "HEINZELMÄNNCHEN" IN COLOGNE.
...THEY BUILD THE DOM...
IT'S ABOUT LITTLE CREATURES THAT DO ALL THE WORK FOR THE PEOPLE...
...AND WE WILL HAVE ACCOMPLISHED OUR TASK...
BECAUSE THE DOM WILL BE COMPLETED!
Wine Tavern
...UNTIL ONE DAY A TAILOR'S WIFE WANTED TO KNOW WHAT WAS GOING ON...
Tailor
WOULD YOU LIKE SOME PEAS?
PEAS
NO, I HAD A LOOK AROUND.
DO YOU THINK THEY'RE WORKING ON THE DOM? THEY'RE IN THEIR BEDS AND SLEEPING!
SHE PUT DOWN SOME PEAS AND THE HEINZELMÄNNCHEN SLIPPED ON THEM.
THEN WE MIGHT AS WELL LEAVE THIS HERE!
PEAS

THE HEINZELMÄNNCHEN TUMBLED DOWN THE STAIRS AND, ANNOYED, THEY LEFT THE TOWN.
Tailor
DRISS!
LET'S GO INSIDE, I BADLY NEED A KÖLSCH!
früh
WHAT IS KÖLSCH ACTUALLY?
The brewery "Früh" was founded in 1904 by Peter Josef Früh. Here you can get traditional Kölsch, but also hearty meals such as crispy knuckle of pork, Cologne Caviar.* Früh's potato soup and, on Tuesdays, fresh potato fritters.
früh KÖLSCH
A TOP-FERMENTED...
...LIGHT...
...HIGHLY FERMENTED...
...HOPS ACCENTUATED...
...CLEAR...
...TASTY BEER...
...STRICTLY BREWED ACCORDING TO THE GERMAN PURITY LAW OF 1516...
...SERVED IN 'TEST TUBES'...
...AND EXCEPTIONALLY SMOOTH!
AND IF YOU REALLY MUST KNOW, THE TERM "KÖLSCH" WAS FIRST USED IN ADVERTISING IN 1918...
...AND IN 1997 THE EU INCLUDED IT IN THE CIRCLE OF PROTECTED REGIONAL SPECIALTIES, JUST LIKE CHAMPAGNE OR COGNAC.
YOU NEED TO VISIT THE REST ROOM.
?
?
I...
I'LL JOIN YOU!
THAT WOMEN ALWAYS HAVE TO GO THE REST ROOM TOGETHER, WAS THAT ALSO YOU...
NO...
...BUT IT WORKS!
HERE, YOUR HALVE HAHN.**
Oh NO, THEY EAT BIRDS LIKE ME IN HERE?

* Blood Sausage with onion,
** Halve Hahn = literally means 'half a rooster'.

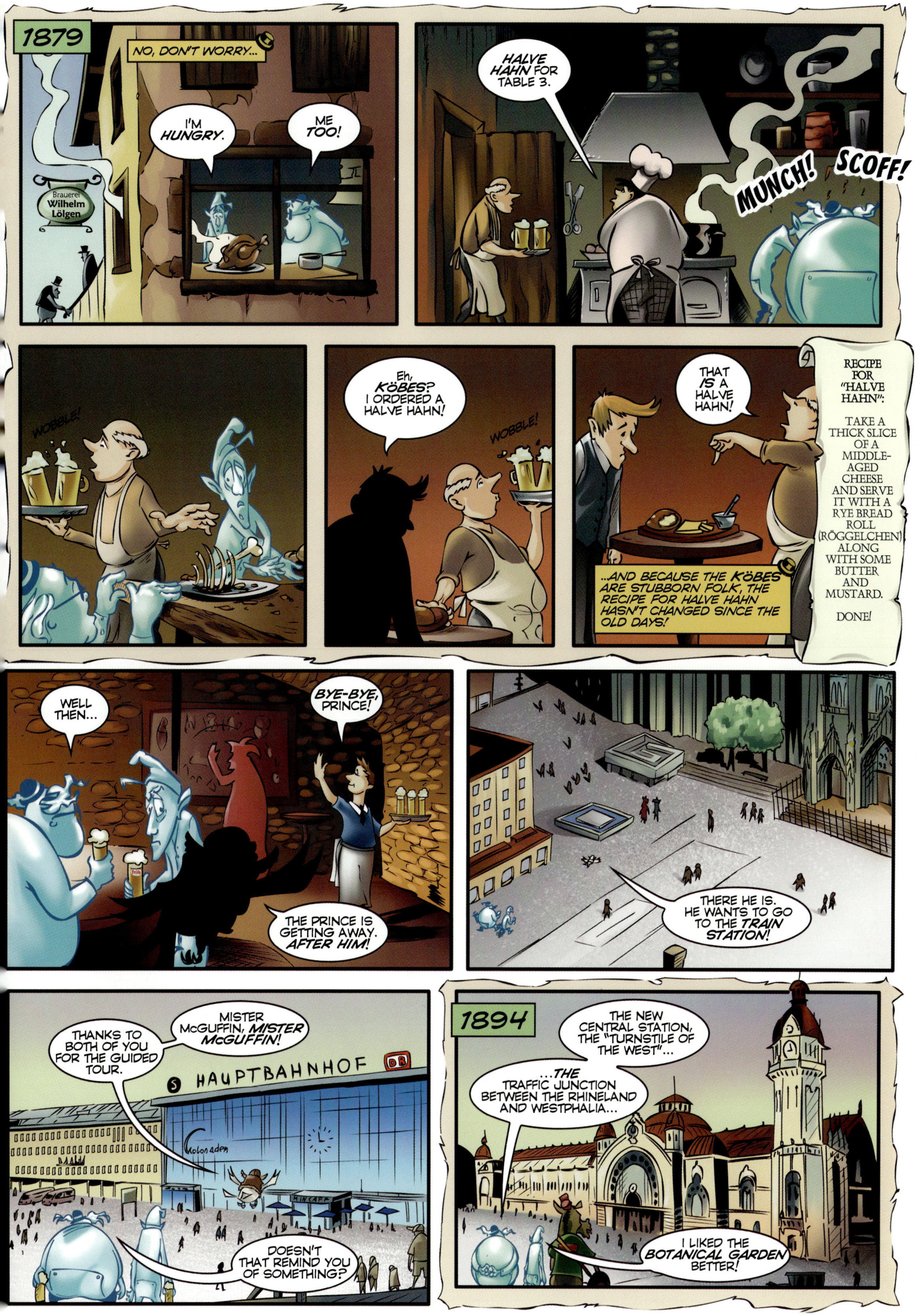
1879
NO, DON'T WORRY...
Brauerei Wilhelm Lölgen
I'M HUNGRY.
ME TOO!
HALVE HAHN FOR TABLE 3.
MUNCH!
SCOFF!
WOBBLE!
Eh, KÖBES? I ORDERED A HALVE HAHN!
WOBBLE!
THAT IS A HALVE HAHN!
...AND BECAUSE THE KÖBES ARE STUBBORN FOLK, THE RECIPE FOR HALVE HAHN HASN'T CHANGED SINCE THE OLD DAYS!
RECIPE FOR "HALVE HAHN": TAKE A THICK SLICE OF A MIDDLE-AGED CHEESE AND SERVE IT WITH A RYE BREAD ROLL (RÖGGELCHEN) ALONG WITH SOME BUTTER AND MUSTARD. DONE!
WELL THEN...
BYE-BYE, PRINCE!
THE PRINCE IS GETTING AWAY. AFTER HIM!
THERE HE IS. HE WANTS TO GO TO THE TRAIN STATION!
THANKS TO BOTH OF YOU FOR THE GUIDED TOUR.
MISTER McGUFFIN, MISTER McGUFFIN!
HAUPTBAHNHOF
DOESN'T THAT REMIND YOU OF SOMETHING?
1894
THE NEW CENTRAL STATION, THE "TURNSTILE OF THE WEST"...
...THE TRAFFIC JUNCTION BETWEEN THE RHINELAND AND WESTPHALIA...
I LIKED THE BOTANICAL GARDEN BETTER!

THAT'S.. ONE OF THE MOST MONUMENTAL BUILDINGS OF ITS KIND!
FANTASTIC! 255 METERS LONG, 64 METERS WIDE...
THAT'S THE LARGEST SINGLE SPAN OF A STATION CONCOURSE ON THE EUROPEAN CONTINENT.
4711
EAU DE COLOGNE
THE STEAM IS RUINING OUR DOM, YOU DO REALIZE THAT.
Oh, YOU OLD MOANER. IT'S SIMPLY A WONDERFUL BUILDING!
HAUPTBAHNHOF
DB
Oh WELL, SHAME WHAT THEY MADE OF IT!
NOW THEN...
ACCORDING TO MY CALCULATIONS WE NEARLY MADE IT.
YOU MEAN...
YES! WE DID IT. OUR TIME IS UP, WE HAVE PAID OUR DEBT TO THE ARCHBISHOP.
IF NOTHING GOES WRONG NOW...
TO OUR FREEDOM!
POFF!!
POFF!!
THE END

Sources:

„Kölsch von A bis Z“, Band 2, Willy Leson, 2001, J.P. Bachem Verlag
„Illustrierte Geschichte der Stadt Köln“, Arnold Stelzmann/Robert Frohn, 1958, 10. Auflage 1984, Bachem
„Das neuzeitliche Köln“, Werner Jung, 2004, Bachem Verlag
„Das mittelalterliche Köln“, Carl Dietmar, 2004, J.P. Bachem Verlag
„Chronik zur Geschichte der Stadt Köln“, Band 1 und 2, 1990, Greven Verlag Köln

Master Illustrations:

Aachen - Etching by Peters
Koblenz - Etching by Peters
Mainz - Etching by Peters
Magdeburg - Etching by Bruck